High strung ar

Penny J Bond

High strung and a bit wild

Penny J Bond

My dog Ruby, who sat by my side when I started this, giving me reassuring looks that my shoulder ache, finger ache and headache will somehow create something unusual and maybe witty.
She can no longer see (this is how long it has taken me to finish this) but she is still always by my side x

High strung and a bit wild   Penny J Bond

Table of contents

Part five

The hardest thing in life is being a vegetarian (and hating mushrooms)
Real friend Vs Pretend friend

Part six

Pet Peeves part one
Questions I ask
Pet Peeves part two
Emails I would prefer not to receive

Part seven

The London Underground System
How to deal with a broken heart My dog hates me
(the personality of a Shar-Pei)
Questions Unanswered
43 things I can't live without
35 things I can live without

Part eight

The Dark Tunnel
A Promise is Forever

Part nine

Part ten

High strung and a bit wild

Penny J Bond

Part one

The Platform of Regret

Have you ever missed a train?

If you have, then you will recognise the feelings you will experience trying to catch it. The mad rush, the sweat, the sheer panic pulsating throughout your entire body, the adrenaline, the lack of oxygen, you push your body past its limits as you race for the train to the destination of your dreams. It starts with the journey there, you know you're pushing it, it's close to departure time and trains don't wait for anyone, you get itchy in the car ride, impatience starts to crawl all over your body, and you have contracted a nervous twitch.

You arrive at the station without remembering how you left the car and you run, somehow managing to read the departures board whilst dashing upstairs to get to your platform. You didn't realise you had such good eyesight or that you could multitask in such a way. It feels as though there are thousands of still lifeless passengers dead set on getting in your way, and you circle through them like your racing through a maze, sweeping in and out of everybody, you jump over hurdles of suitcases like you're fighting for gold at the Olympics.

Everything is becoming frantic, but with a glimmer of hope you see the big number looming over the platform, you just need to reach it, it's there, it's within your grasp. Just keep running, you're against the clock, it doesn't matter that you have somehow forgotten how to breathe during this moment, you can catch your breath when you get there.

As you race to the finish line you see the door of opportunity you plan to propel yourself into, you slow down because you think you're there and then suddenly without any warning the door slams shut, this train is not for you.

You're halted, your entire body does an emergency stop. You stand in bewilderment, you tried your hardest, or so you think you did, it was just right there, close enough for you to touch. The cold sweat starts trickling down your neck, everything has suddenly slowed down to a pace that's slower than slow. As the train starts to pull away, you see the faces of the smug passengers, who just witnessed your feeble attempt at joining them, they know you'll be left on the platform of regret, alone with all the other regrets in life, maybe these passengers have been where you are, but not today

for they raced against time and they won, but for
you it was too late, you left it too late!

As the train veers out of the distance, everything
suddenly becomes eerily quiet, the only sound you
can hear is your deep breath, as you try to replace
all of the oxygen you just lost, and your ears are
alerted to how everything has suddenly fallen
silent, it's that quiet you can hear the thumping of
your heart as the blood pulsates through it. The
silence that has surrounded you is for you, for you
to reminisce, reminisce about trying harder, what if
you had pushed yourself more? what if you had
left sooner rather than later?

The cauldron black crows are all lined on the
fence, their eyes fixated on you as though they are
looking into your soul, they have no words for
you, they too have fallen silent, they have watched
this moment replayed a million times, they will
allow you time to find solace in the silence that
surrounds you, they don't want to break your
concentration at this moment in time. As you
slump on the bench that resides on the platform of
regret, you look back on your life, it's this moment
that defines all of the times in your life when you
could have succeeded. If only you had tried harder
and leapt for that door, for that door is every
opportunity you could have had. But you were

lazy, and you took your time, you forgot that time expires, you don't get it back, you can't rewind and replay, it doesn't work that way, and you didn't fight hard enough, for what you wanted, you really wanted that train.

Now, as you sit alone with your cold sweat and your heavy breathing, you can decide how to live your life moving forward, you can take chances and be there when the opportunities are waiting for you, you can make the decision to not let them pass you by, or you can live on a loop of missing that train, but this platform is not a place you want to keep visiting, it's cold and eerie and consumed by regret…where you're all alone, except for the cauldron black crows who are deciding on whether they'll see you again anytime soon…

The Dinted tin

You know the one, that's left on the supermarket shelf. I bet nine times out of ten you move the dinted tin and reach all the way to the back for a perfectly shaped one. No-one wants the imperfect one, they want the one that isn't broken, they want the one that looks how it should, how the factory intended it to be manufactured.

Have you ever left the item because the whole box is full of dinted tins? Have you swapped to another brand as these tins aren't dinted, admit it have you done this? Now, why are you reaching for the perfect looking one? That tin may be dinted, and its been bashed about a bit on its journey, but once that tin is open, the contents will be the same as the perfect looking one. It is also fair to say that I have picked up a perfect tin, still in date, and once home and open, it was mouldy inside. My eyes were alerted to the furry substance, the colour of a crystal-clear ocean and my brain immediately set off sirens and reacted to - this is not how it should be! Now, would that have happened with the dinted one, if I had of picked that one up? this is a question I will never get an answer too. I didn't give the dinted tin a chance, I went on looks alone.

The moral to this is, imagine that dinted tin is a person you are choosing and not a tin of food. If you go through life solely looking for perfect on the outside and not looking at what's in the inside, or even considering what journey that person has been on up to this point ,to explain why they are a little damaged on the outside, then you may just be left with a bad taste in your mouth.
Just that…

The Doctor's Waiting Room

You must have been in a doctor's waiting room and observed how the waiting system is.

Sometimes you can be sat there for what feels like forever. You double check in your mind if you signed in correctly, did the receptionist take the right name, because you see people come in a lot later than you, but they are seen first and in the blink of an eye they have continued on with their day, whilst you're losing valuable time in this musty room, reading the same health warning posters on the wall and eyeballing the same people from across the room, whilst trying to block out that person with the annoying cough and the drone of the telephone, from more patients ringing in for their share of the attention.

You're getting impatient, the foot tapping starts and rises to an extent you may not realise how loud that tap is becoming. Your fingers are twitching, I am not sure why we do this, it makes no difference to the situation, but all of a sudden involuntary body actions have begun, even the clearing of the throat several times like you're ready to scream out at the next patient that walks through the door, to declare to them you was here first and you're not going after them, this is a fact. You're ready for a fight with anyone and everyone at this point.

You check your watch, your clock on your phone and the clock on the wall at least thirty times in the space of one minute, because you're questioning why this process works this way, was I early? Was I late? Is that patient more important than me? have they forgotten about me? who came up with this system? Time is ticking by, tick, tick, tick and you're now wondering why you thought it would be a good idea to fit this appointment in when you have places to be, but you're not going anywhere anytime soon, because when you look up from checking your phone for the forty fifth time you see there is now suddenly more patients in the waiting room.

So many so, that there are no seats left and now it's lets play musical chairs on who needs the seat more, obviously the elderly lady Doris, who has been walking across the doctors car park since you first got seated needs the chair, and you know her journey just across the car park has taken this amount of time, because when you were not checking the time from every source possible, you occasionally glanced out of the window and was subconsciously cheering her on, hoping you would eventually see her get to the finish line.

So, now you don't even have a comfortable seat to be impatient in, and your anger has turned to rage inside, you want to go over to the receptionist and rip into her about how long you've waited and how many people have gone in before you ,and you want an apology from her, when she explains she didn't actually check you in, this happens because she has so many patients in the room and you must have been missed, but at the same time you don't want to expose your rage in front of the overcrowded waiting room, you're not ready for your fifteen minutes of fame, although you may receive a standing ovation, because you have now noticed there are still other patients sitting there from you came in.

You decide maybe you need to take a step back and calm down, if anyone should be up there first it should be one of them. Now you secretly want one of them to look like the villain and go up and scream at her, and when everyone looks shocked and surprised that someone let rage get the better of them, you will be glad you did not overreact that way.

Depending on how long you're waiting, there will come a time where your rage will get the better of you, lets face it, you're not going to wait around forever, regardless of whether the man standing across from you does have perspiration pouring down his face and a neck like a rain fall on an Aprils day, and it's clear that some of the patients in here don't look like they have five minutes left of life inside them.

Now, I'm going to turn this all around and tell you that this whole situation is not about being in the doctor's waiting room, this is what being in debt feels like.

You are trapped in a room that you are cornered in, you can't leave this room because you need this appointment, so you will be trapped here until you are called. Being called is when you're able to pay all of your debts off, and those oh so impatient patients are all creditors and people you owe money too and the longer you make them wait the more rage they get and the more furious they become, to the point where you're now no longer a patient yourself, but you look up and realise that you are actually the receptionist looking around a waiting room full of angry people that have been waiting and waiting a very long time for you to pay them back. Remember how you felt earlier in this room, clock watching, rage inside, getting to the point you'll not wait, you have other business to attend too, that's how every single one of these people feel about you. However, the doctor that can make all of this go away is in fact money and without it these people won't be leaving anytime soon. It's not a nice situation to be in, not everyone causes this themselves, one day they're full of life completely healthy and then from out of nowhere debt comes along, maybe one day something needed fixing, maybe it was the dog and the endless vet bills, maybe it was the car that you needed for work that broke down, and suddenly one situation can spiral everything out of control. You thought you had it all worked out and then there you are with a queue that is building and building its way out of the door and no one is waiting, there are demands coming from every corner, and how do you sort it when everyone wants now, the doctor can only see one person at a time, the only way you can sort this is to prioritise the sick from the ones who will need to wait, this is how I look at my finances and it happens to all of us at some point in our lives.

Tapping Bird

I haven't always got things right in my life, in fact I have got so many things wrong. I won't blame anyone or any circumstances, but I will say the choices I made to do the wrong things, probably wouldn't have happened if my circumstances were different. However, I have to accept that whatever I was going through, I made the decision to make these mistakes and I can't change these things, but I have learnt from them, how I act today is based on those mistakes for I knew they were wrong and I don't want to burn myself again, because regret hurts, it plays on your mind like a little bird tapping away at your inner brain and you can't get the bird out, because once you made that mistake, you placed that bird in there and they don't intend on ever moving out. So think carefully, think before you act and ask yourself, is this something that will put a constant tapping bird inside my head, and if you make more than one mistake then you will be adding more and more birds, until the day you can no longer focus on life or comprehend what you want out of life, because the knocking will always be there and it will get louder and louder the older you get.

No-one is perfect, we will always make mistakes, but just ensure your mistakes are little ones, normal ones that we should all make, not big ones that affect other peoples lives, because it's the guilt from affecting someone else that brings that bird to your brain. And if you do make mistakes, then learn from them, if you can learn from them, then at least when you close your eyes at the end of the day the bird won't be aggressively tapping, it will just be a humming tap in the background overshadowed by your days thoughts.

There is a reason we make mistakes and that is to learn from them, because if we didn't make errors then how would we ever understand what we want out of life or who we are. If you do make a mistake and it's too late to realise what you have done, then it's ok too, we all do it, and sometimes things are out of our hands. Don't beat yourself up too much, that bird is tapping not judging.

Don't let it eat you away, redeem yourself by once again learning from it, if you repeat these mistakes then you will only have yourself to blame and sympathy won't come knocking, just that bird will…

Part two

Dear Diary

February 25

I can't stand my boss. I physically despise her.

The things that go through my mind when I think of how I could shut her up permanently. I feel I am committing a crime just by plotting this secretly in my thoughts. The most dangerous side comes out of me when I hear her voice, it goes straight through my insides with a hacksaw. I have thought of no less than 27 ways to dispose of her and get away with it.

She is the definition of evil. I now watch the crime channel nightly to get tips on how to get away with this should this situation actually take place. I am sure no-one would miss her, and I am sure her 1st friend when she arrives in Hell would be Hitler. Friend request already accepted. I imagine them plotting together if they ever get the chance to be re-born. 40 hours a week no less I have to tolerate her bull S***, her pretend niceness when the bigger boss comes by, the way she belittles everyone but smiles while she does it, so it's meant to be a nice insult.

Her fake happiness gets me the most, why isn't she living in a musical for villains.

I hate her clothing.

She has fat feet and fat shoes

She needs to wash her hair sometimes and drink less coffee.

I imagine her being demoted and the person she has been the most-evil too taking over her job. Steve the office admin guy, he would most certainly get revenge on her if he was boss, he looks like a secret serial killer. She has caused him more problems than anyone else, he has become a nervous wreck in her presence, but really, he is waiting for the perfect moment to get his sweet justice and put her head on a plate.

I hate her makeup; she looks like an evil clown and that positively vile scent of odour la slut she wears.

What did I do to end up with her as a boss?

The worst part, the other bosses love her.

I am not quitting she will love that.

Bitch!

March 4

We have a new girl in our office who has just transferred from another office in our company. I hate her! She and bitch boss seem very friendly. She eats all day and says "ohhhh I can just eat and eat and never put weight on" this makes me sick. How did she end up with this privilege being such a knob? I look at a biscuit and two stone is automatically added to my arse.

I hate her face; it has cracks from the days old foundation she is wearing.

She buys expensive clothes and pretends she is rich. She isn't, she shags anything that moves and makes them buy her stuff, so she doesn't tell their wives.

I heard her new car came from one of the higher bosses because she sucked him off in the canteen toilets.

Her voice kills me inside.

I want her to wake up tomorrow and realise her vagina has closed up.

How you going to get your expensive clothes now.

Infact lets close her mouth up as well, she seems to use this more than her vagina, so I have heard.

When she is flirting with everyone I imagine smashing her head through the computer screen over and over again. I have stalked her social networking, I am sick of the same photos of her lunch time banquet fit for a king and the same skinny poses she does, F***ing pig.

I wonder if anyone else feels the same hate towards her as I do.

F***ing prostitute.

Why do I have to sit next to her, I am sure I have caught Chlamydia from being this close to her.

April 29

Tonight, I am sitting with my blinds drawn. My phone is tightly in my grips and I have a baseball bat next to my feet. I am scared, scared for my life.

Earlier today I went to see my reflexologist. The last time I went I left bad feedback as she was constantly talking about herself and ruining my calm time. I came away with a headache rather than inner peaceful feelings. I feel due to the stress at work I need me time. It's the only time I can switch off and not think about the absolute morons I spend 40 hours a week with.

So, it was awkward going in as I know she will have seen my feedback and I was hoping she would take something from this and stop talking about her problems to me. But this time was different than I expected. She was extremely happy with me, overly nice, you know those people that you know want to secretly kill you, but they put that fake happy expression on, only they go too far, and this really grinds me. So, I just went with it and thought I would once again leave bad feedback,until the idiot is finally replaced with someone who just shuts up.

During my hour session with her, she constantly talked as expected once again. Only this time it seemed more threats than friendly chat. She told me about her boss, "**Don**" and how mad he gets if she receives bad feedback. So, she is going to ensure she doesn't receive this in future, as it's not what her "**family**" want for her. I sat in silence as usual just absorbing the information she was spilling out at me. But when she mentioned the feedback again, I felt I had to say something to her. I apologised about leaving it and explained I just need quiet time, and she told me to "**forget about it**".

She laughed hysterically and told me there is no hard feelings, that she understands she is very chatty and it's not like she is going to "**whack**" me or something over it. She then went on to talk about her week and how she has been very busy "**spring cleaning**". It was at this point I started wondering what exactly she was trying to say to me in that cheery tone of hers. I started to feel somewhat uncomfortable and started counting down how long I had left in this session. She also apologised about making me feel uncomfortable the previous time and said, "If I am too rough tell me, it's not like I **pinched you** or anything"? I had 35 minutes of this left and I felt it was becoming somewhat hostile in there. I explained I may need to leave early as I need to go pick something up from the shop and she asked me if I needed to collect "an outfit" I wasn't too sure what she was suggesting and I said no, I need to fetch some "**juice**" as I have ran out. I told her I was feeling quite "**heavy**" and the juice helped me. She asked me if I "**eat alone**" and I wasn't sure why she was asking me this, so I said no I usually eat at work with "**the boss**", she told me she was seeing her "**boss**" after the session and it was at this point I was starting to piece all the sub text she had gone through with me during the session.

She said after work she was going to spend the evening playing with her "**rat**" and at this point I excused myself as I had a lot to do that day. I didn't leave any feedback and couldn't get out of there quick enough, I apologised and again she told me to "**forget about it**" and I left with my shoe hanging off my foot.

When I arrived home, I checked all my windows and doors were locked and shut my blinds. I think my reflexologist is a gangster and I am expecting her to arrive at mine tonight. I will not take this laying down, I am sitting here waiting for her.

Gosh, all this over some feedback. I contemplated if I am being paranoid, but I have seen enough gangster films to know she means business. I am trying so hard to stay awake, but damn her reflexology is starting to kick in. This could be my last entry…

May 5
So far nothing has happened, and no one has come to my house. I am wondering if they are playing it cool and if the mob will arrive at mine when I least

expect it. This morning I received a letter from the spa, requesting I find another reflexologist as the one I saw the other day is now fully booked moving forward for the next six months. I thought this was very strange that they didn't want my business and I am confused by this letter, is this all part of their ploy to use the element of surprise.

I have looked online and there are weekly Yoga sessions at the local gym, so I am going to try that on Thursday, that's if I am still here.

May 13

I am 100% never going back to that gym. That Yoga class was appalling. I have put in a massive complaint about the teacher and his disgusting method of teaching. I feel as though I have lost any self-esteem I may have had before walking into that room. I don't want to go too much into it, as I feel very embarrassed about the entire thing. I am hoping the teacher gets the sack for how he has singled me out and treated me.

Within 5 minutes of being there he looked at me and said this move is called the "**cow face pose**" cow face what on earth was he suggesting, that was harsh after only knowing me for 5 minutes. I went bright red and felt completely picked on. What a horrible little man!

He then came across to me and showed me the "easy pose" I am not sure what he has heard about me, but I certainly do not need to know about a pose like this, the cheeky B*****d. I felt everyone in the room was a part of this as they all kept smiling at me. Who smiles when someone is being so cruel to someone, I felt bullied by the entire room.

We did some more moves where he didn't single me out, but the icing on the cake for me, was when he came over and performed the "**downward dog pose**" well I just got up, rolled up my mat, threw it on the pile of stale mats that appear to have never been washed down, declared I am unsure why he feels insulting me is acceptable. I looked at the rest of the class and told them they should all feel ashamed by joining in on the bullying and they just sat there laughing which made me angrier. I turned to that disgusting human being and told him I will be putting in a complaint about him and that if I have a "cow face" then he has a cat's ass face!!!! I slammed the door on my way out to disturb their calm feelings and went straight to the reception desk, who didn't seem to take my complaint seriously, I explained it appears that the Yoga instructor is a sex pest/woman hater and they told me to put it in writing.

So, that is exactly what I am in the middle of doing! When I walked out of the entrance, I could hear the receptionists laughing, so I will be including them in my complaint as well the snide little b*****s. It's disgraceful behaviour and I wouldn't want anyone else to experience that first-hand! I feel the past week has not been the best week for me…

Part three

If our paths cross

Her

If our paths cross, I would tell him how amazing he is.

If our paths cross, I would tell him how much I am inspired by him.

If our paths cross, I would tell him how special he is. How would I tell him? with my eyes and not my lips. No speech would come out to say these words. I would delicately tell him with the gentleness of my eyes that would say I am so interested in you. I would look past his eyes and into his soul and softly wrap my arms around it and tell it that it's the most beautiful soul I have seen.

I would smile with my eyes in a girly way and my eyelashes would give a gentle flutter occasionally, with their nod of approval. I would give him a curled-up smile, but at the same time a seriousness would be behind my eyes, because I would want him to know I mean every non spoken word of this.

I would savour every single second of his beautiful adoring eyes and capture a photograph with my mind of how delightful his smile is, to remind me on days if our paths don't ever cross again just how beautiful he is.

I would hang on every word he says to me. I would hush the butterflies that are circling my inner self to stay calm and I would pinch myself to keep my nerves steady. I would assert my brain into not saying anything that is not necessary, and I would keep my speech to small amounts of words if I have to speak, so as not to burst open with all my inner thoughts and feelings.

I would want to tell him everything about myself, but I won't, because it would come out as an explosion of language attacking his sweet soul.

I wouldn't tell him about the times I have crossed paths with him before.

Like the day he looked so on edge and nervous, he sat pinching his hand and whatever was going through his mind, it was clearly troubling him, and I wanted to go to him and wrap my arms around him and protect him from whatever was making him feel so lost and gently kiss his battered hand that was turning snow white from the lack of blood getting to it.

I wouldn't tell him about the time, he sat smiling and laughing and it lit up my entire day, there was something special about his beaming smile that stayed with me until dusk set in. I wouldn't tell him that nothing else was important that day as everything seemed prettier when I reflected on that laugh of his and how all the worlds floors I walked on that day seemed somewhat bouncy.

I also wouldn't tell him about the time I over-heard his conversation and I was stunned at how intelligent another human could be. How I sat bewildered on how much he knew and the words he used and how much this impressed me and made me want to induce more of him and his vocabulary that was like another language which is yet to be discovered.

I wouldn't tell him how he is always on my mind and I wonder whether right at this moment he is smiling and making other peoples days light up or whether he is feeling lost like that day not so long ago.

I wouldn't tell him how when people are talking to me all I see is his beautiful eyes and I cannot see anything beyond this now. I have his image imprinted into my soul, and my work has now declined, because I no longer concentrate on everyday tasks like I used to.

I wonder if he has someone special and whether they feel this way towards him or whether they are blinded by his beauty. I wonder how I will move past this and if I will ever feel this way towards another human being.

I wonder if this is what love at first sight feels like and will my life become a sentence of what if's? I wonder if I was destined to meet him and whether my future will have him in it?

I wonder if I will ever have human contact with him and how my body would feel to be touched by him? His beautiful hands, his gentle looking fingers, my body feels electrified just thinking about this with every single hair standing to attention.

His hair has changed recently, and he looks more and more beautiful every-time I see him. I imagine running my fingers through his hair and smiling at him with my eyes and my heart beats so fast I lose my breath. What I would do to ruffle his hair like a mountain of feathers at my fingertips.

I wonder if he has ever seen me before and what would be going through his mind when his eyes catch mine. My eyes never lie, will he see through my stare to the bottom of my inner feelings and I will be revealed and exposed.

What would be his first impression of me? would it be good feelings? would I light up his day somewhat? Would he be a human lie detector and prove that the expensive perfume I am wearing was purchased after the first encounter I had with him, just on the off chance we met again. Then there is the make-up I now apply for him, in the hope he will see me and think she looks beautiful, and the delicately polished manicure I have now which was inspired by him.

Would he remember I used to wear flat shoes before, and now I wear sleek high heels that I struggle to wear all day just so he can get a glimpse of my pencil thin legs.

I wonder if I will finally stop being punished, and that my heart could take a day off from over beating when he is in my presence and that one day, he will come up to me and say "hello" for I am too scared to act on my impulses.

I wish on every star I see in the sky at night and I have now become an avid stargazer. The trains arrived, he isn't here yet, I wonder where he is.

Him

If our paths cross, there are so many things I would say to you.

I would say how you light up my day with your beautiful face and your endearing smile. I would say to you that from the first time I caught sight of you, I haven't been able to think of anything but you. I would say to you, that I am struggling to keep these feelings in, and I fear I will eventually burst.

I would say to you, that I find it hard to focus on anything since my eyes found yours and how I have never been so fixated on anyones eyes like I am yours. How I try so hard to make eye contact with you, but I find it difficult. I am afraid you will see straight through me and into my heart or even my soul. I fear you will see all over my face that I find you to be completely mesmerising and I can't imagine not seeing your eyes every-day.

I would say that once I tried so hard to talk to you, I practiced our introduction all morning, but when the time came, my heart filled up and it became so

overwhelming that first introduction. I became
weak and somewhat lost and became a mess. My
inner self was kicking at me to man up, but my
legs were like jelly and I sat pinching my hand to
bring my pulse back down to earth. I suddenly
started sweating and my breath became shorter and
I hope you didn't see me this day. I fear you saw
me this day in this way. I hope you didn't.

I would say to you, that those high heels you are
wearing are making me crazy. I would ask that you
go back to your flat shoes, for I cannot get those
heels out of my mind and you the essence of
beauty in those heels is very distracting to me.
Those heels are making it harder for me to
approach you.

I would say that I sit for hours and hours through
the day wondering if you have someone special.
How can someone so beautiful not have someone
to love or to be loved by.

I would say that I can smell you hours after seeing
you, with that completely enticing scent you wear.

I would say to you, that I have never felt this way
towards anyone in my entire life (and I find my
behaviour quite embarrassing) and I fear I never
will again. I fear I will spend my life trying to find
you if I lose sight of you.

I would say to you that I am trying so hard to impress you, but you don't seem to be noticing. I use my word of the day in every single mornings conversations, because I want you to hear and think I am somewhat intelligent.

I have grown my hair because this style seems to be in recently. I dress somewhat smarter in the hope I impress you and these shirts are hard to iron.

I would say "hello" to you and you would want to talk to me and all these inner self doubts would be washed away and I could get round to requesting you to dinner, because I have imagined this scene and played it out in my head a thousand times, the moment I get your undivided attention and I get to learn all about you, this mysterious beautiful woman I am so drawn too.

I would sit and be the silent listener absorbing all the delicious words that are created by your beautiful lips which have become more redder recently and I also find this distracting. What I would do to press my lips on yours and feel your inner breath. To run my fingers through your hair and stare into those crystal blue pools that you have been blessed with. I would say to you, that one day I am going to tell you all the above. I am going to be brave and bite the bullet or I will live with this regret my whole life, feeling miserable I let the most stunning vision fade away. I would tell you that February the 14th was created for you, however cheesy that may sound.

But today is not that day for I missed the train, maybe tomorrow.

Being blessed with a bitch face

So, for a long time or rather since birth I have been blessed with this beautiful piece of artwork called the "Bitch Face". Here is my advice on surviving in a hostile world with a hostile face. Not everyone is blessed with this, others have the relaxed and approachable face, they have to do very little with their expression and people can see they have a gentle or nice nature just from the first impression of meeting them. However this couldn't be further from someone who constantly looks as though they are chewing a bee or an entire hive depending on how unfortunate you were. Here's what I have found from looking this way.

Cons

1) People are going to be intimidated by you
2) People will think you don't like them instantly

3) You are going to have a lot of people dislike you, just from your face
4) You may or may not get punched in a club, because you looked at someone the wrong way
5) Your boss is always going to wonder if you like working where you are, because you never look happy
6) Your partners are always going to question if they are actually making you happy because from the outer look it doesn't appear to be the case
7) You may get deleted on social networks because your profile photo is giving your friend a dirty look
8) You will drive fear into those who are completely baffled as to what they have done, just from the dirty looks you constantly hand out to them
9) You may get called a miserable bitch by employees and friends of friends, who always comment on how angry you appear
10) You may not get jobs because your face is just too hostile
11) New friendships are always going to be hard work, until you prove yourself
12) You are going to spend a lot of your life saying "It's just my face"
13) Your arguments with people will erupt very quickly, because you have no idea the anger rays your face is beaming off

14) No-one in your life is ever going to buy you a "Little miss ray of sunshine" cup for any occasion

15) You will receive different customer service because the salesperson already feels threatened by you, without having to try to upsell you something as well

16) You're going to be involved in a lot of misunderstood situations

17) People will ask you a lot of the time "are you ok" "you look mad/p***** off?"

18) Your life will be filled with having to explain to everyone on a daily basis you're fine

19) People will double look at you, trying to find out why you just death stared at them, if you don't appreciate attention you may struggle with this

20) You're going to find it hard to find a relationship where the other person understands all the above

21) You are going to have people think you are not genuine, because you say something heartfelt with an expression that says "You're going to die later, mark my words"

Ok so the above gives an outline, it doesn't barely scratch the surface on the problems someone with this face endures on a daily basis, so let's look at some of the pro's.

Pros

1) People won't want to mess with you from instantly meeting you
2) You will always look younger than those around you, because your facial muscles are working 24 hours a day to keep that face looking tight (no Botox needed)
3) You may get jobs just because the interviewer will fear repercussion if they don't hire you
4) When people get to know you and they see past your face, they will love you, because your pretty awesome, in fact no you are the most awesome person they know
5) Customer service people will deal with complaints quicker, they don't want trouble
6) Your mum will always make sure you get extra attention to your other siblings because she doesn't like seeing you look sad, expect additional Christmas gifts!
7) So, what if you intimidate future partners, but do you really want them approaching you if they have insides made up of washing up bubbles
8) You will always wear the trousers in relationships, the face says so
9) Be glad people delete you off social networking, saves you a job and makes you look the bigger person
10) When you have children, they will read your expression and people with bitch faces generally only need to tell their children once

11) Peoples first impressions of you are, you can look after yourself and you end up with a reputation that couldn't be farther from the truth

12) If you ever audition for a Pantomime, chances are you would get the Villain part without having to pick the script up

13) You will always intimidate others without even knowing it

14) People love a moody looking model

15) When you send someone an angry emoji, they know you mean it

16) People in lifts and waiting rooms may talk to you, because they are nervous or fear you

17)You don't get laughter lines like everyone else

18) You don't have to put the duck pout on

19) If someone was debating on attacking you while you're walking home at 4am, your face tells them your trained in mixed martial arts and they will re-think that decision, you have probably been saved on countless occasions you just don't realise it

20) People will go out of their way to make you smile, if they don't know you, be prepared to be surrounded by jesters and you're the Queen.

So, summing it up, although it can feel like a curse on certain days, it's not actually that bad, just embrace your face, it's yours, and if people don't understand you, then they don't know you.

Ride it out

Life is a rollercoaster they say, there will be twists and turns and certainly rocky patches.

You are bound to encounter experiences that launch you out of your seat. Nobody stands over you when you're younger and tells you to ensure you stay buckled in. The advice we do get, is although those rocky turns will seem like the end for you, they won't be. Because sure enough that turn will be followed by a slide of better times.

The moral is, stay seated, keep on that ride. The day you take yourself off it, you will have left the ride of your life. Some experiences on it may seem dark and scary and there will always be that tunnel where you hold on so tight your knuckles turn white. But you will see the light at the end and be rest assured the light will be there waiting for you again. When you go up that ramp to the highest heights, you will be terrified to face that drop. But know that when you get to the bottom of that drop, you will question how brave you were to face that fear in the first place.

You will survive everything this ride puts you through and although it's always easiest to remember the scary and sad moments, there will be lots of laugh out loud and lose your breath moments included. The more times you go around that ride, the easier it will feel.

The first drop may feel the scariest, but you will become immune to situations that were more than terrifying the first time around.

During your ride, you will see familiar faces and feel secure knowing you're not alone. But at some point, these people will leave the ride, and you will feel a deep sadness. But this is life it's inevitable and something that is out of your control. Not everybody will stay on your ride throughout your life, they have other places to go, and they too have lost people on their journey. But be assured others will then join the ride and they'll never replace those who left, but they will be there to support you once again.

The only thing you can do is ride it out. Be prepared for unexpected moments, and don't ever take yourself off the ride. No matter how low you feel or lost. There are always others seated on your ride who may not always feel as though they see how lost you are, but they're there, you never ride on the rollercoaster as a single rider.

Wake up and look around, you are surrounded by others. If you feel it's too much, reach out and one of them will hold your hand until you pass that dark tunnel again. When you reach the end of the ride and it's your time to leave, then embrace all of those moments you survived through.

Be thankful you got to experience it and you shared it with all those that love you. Stand tall that you didn't quit, and you stayed and experienced every single emotion that ride gave you.

But the most important part of the ride, is enjoy it, it won't last forever, at some point everything has to stop, and there may be times when the ride needs maintenance work and you need to take a time out, but you will get back on it again, just believe in your own strength and keep fighting to stay on it and ride it out…

Part four

The Automatic Chip Policy

From the 1st of October 2027, every single person born in this Country will have a chip inserted into them. Everyone else on this day will receive a date they'll be able to attend to have theirs inserted.

This chip can be scanned to prove how old this person is. It will also be updated when this person has a sexually transmitted disease or when this person has a criminal record. It can also tell you if this person is a constant bull s****** and whether they are two faced.

Every person residing in this country ,will automatically be given a free scanner so you can scan anyone to check if they have a good credit report, if they are underage, if they are free of STD's, if they use porn, if they have sexual feelings for your friends or their boss, if they have psychopathic thoughts and whether you want to allow them into the company of your family or your circle of friends.

We are proud our Country can allow its residents to feel safe and for them to know about the people they are friends with.

You no longer have to worry on a first date or when you become friends with someone new about whether you can trust them or not. It is a legal requirement that all residents have this chip inserted.

It is a crime to not attend the date you are given. If you do not have the chip inserted when requested. You will be found, and the chip will be inserted anyway, we WILL load your chip with the worst traits as punishment, so good luck getting laid in the future. It is in your best interest to come along with a positive attitude as this will benefit our future and yours.

For any questions, you may have on this, tough it's a no questions policy.

Kind Regards
The people who run the Country

The New Income Scheme

From the 1st of next month, the Government has implemented a new income scheme for the people.

As requested by the people themselves through many elections and debates. *If you have any questions please feel free to contact your local authority. However most of them will be on holiday for the next 7 weeks due to our in-house benefit package of 7 weeks abroad each year, so you may have to contact them after this time period, where they will still be drunk on happiness from their cruise-ship full of pampering sessions and free bar cocktails, and they will be more than happy to help.

The following schemes have now been put in place in sections, please find the section you fall under and check your status and your entitlement. If you fall into more than one category, we suggest you stop being dishonest and pick the section that is true for you.

The Workers

Anyone that works full time, part time, self-employed, or employed, and this job has at least 35 hours a week, have now been put into the workers income scheme.

From the 1st of next month you will all be entitled to 12 week's annual holiday a year from your employer. This is because you all work extremely hard throughout the year and it's about time you all got to enjoy some downtime, without having to worry about paying your bills. So, your annual leave will now be fully paid. Don't worry about your employer he has no choice, it's the Governments decision not theirs. You can take this holiday at Christmas, on bank holidays, weekends, and school terms. There are no restrictions. Your annual leave will be signed off even if all the staff have chosen the same dates. It is now your employer's problem to hire further staff not yours.

Your income will be increased, confirmation will be sent over shortly, as you are not going to spend your entire life relying on credit because minimum wage is atrocious. Your income will cover all of your outgoings and ensure you have more than enough to live comfortably and be able to afford all those nice treats you are currently paying for on credit.

Your credit cards will be cleared as you shouldn't have ever been put in a position being a worker where you needed to use credit to pay for that broken washing machine, boiler repairs etc. Please fill in the attached form with all of your current debts and these will be cleared within 28 days from receiving them.

Your lunch breaks are now extended to 2 hours daily paid. This is to ensure you have time to visit the Doctors, dentist, pick the kids up, walk the dog, go shopping and then actually have a lunch break. We have understood how stressful your lives have become trying to fit everything in on a daily basis. No more rushing around at lunch for you.

We are lowering tax on your income, because we have understood that a large portion has been taken in the past for pretty useless reasons. Any overtime you work is now tax free, if you're willing to work hard, we will not punish you for it, we will reward you for supporting yourselves and we will no longer be taxing it.

Your student finance debt will be cleared, because we understand that paying for a course that costs £9000 a year for 3 years, was a ridiculous move on our part. University fees are now being lowered back to the £1175 a year amount. But as it was our error, we will accept this and wipe your current debt.

If you have experienced tyre problems getting to work due to endless potholes in the roads, please contact us, we will give you a new car as an apology for the inconvenience caused by us not using your tax money to fix them.

If you have had your rubbish bin left because it was fuller than usual and the lid was open by 5cm or less, please inform us of the date, we will contact the team of rubbish collectors and they will be dismissed for not removing your waste. After all you are paying for this service and if you're not receiving it then heads will roll.

Retirement age has been lowered to 50, let's face it, when your 65-70 there are a lot of things you may not be able to enjoy at retirement age, so were lowering it to ensure it's as fun as you want it to be, and don't worry about pensions, we are going to refer to this in the next section.

Pensions, we have decided to triple the state pension and also make your employer triple your work pension, we will not have any pensioners cold or hungry in the future, you will be able to enjoy growing old with a full belly and a warm house as a thank you for all your years of working.

Benefits, you will no longer be paying for any benefits unemployed people may have received. Please enjoy the pleasure of knowing all of your tax will be used to pay for more security around your areas, providing a safe place for your children to grow up in. We will use the remainder on local charities, building more centres for children, parks, improving public transport and making your communities beautiful places to live.

Everyone will also be receiving a complimentary hover board when they are released in 2030, there will be a hover board party, more details to follow.

Parking Tickets, if you are a worker you will no longer have to pay to park. We realise you work hard and sometimes having a coffee catch up in town can take a little longer than usual. We don't want you hindered by having to rush back to the car park because you may incur a fine, so workers will no longer be required to pay for any parking, anywhere. Please use the workers badge on your dashboard when you park to ensure no ticket is issued. Display it correctly on your dashboard as required.

Christmas bonus, we are ensuring you will all receive a bonus, enough to cover your family's needs during the holidays. We don't want families suffering working long hours to pay for this family holiday. You will receive this bonus at the end of October every year to ensure you have plenty of time to purchase your turkey, decorations and gifts. Happy Holidays. Payment amount details will follow and will be based on your family size and needs.

Clothing allowance, it has now been decided that unemployed people appear to have more designer clothes than the workers. Your monthly clothing allowance will be included in your pay to ensure the workers work that catwalk look and this will also distinguish the non-workers in the crowd. We have calculated this amount from your current age group and your current need to look good, younger workers may receive slightly more than the older workers as they are more concerned with labels.

The Non-workers

For those who are currently not employed, the following changes will take place for you, beginning from the 1st of the month. If you have any questions please don't run around like headless chickens, wait 7 weeks-time and an advisor will be happy to clear up any disgruntles you may have. This section does not include changes for those who are currently not working due to health issues. Please see the next section for your changes.

Benefits - all benefits will stop on the 1st of the month. This is due to you not working, You will now be employed by the Government directly and you will be assigned a job fit for you. If you choose not to accept any of the jobs offered, you will be risking making yourself homeless and we will be unable to help you. The jobs on offer vary and will be assigned to your actual needs and requirements. For examples please see as follows

Gardening for the workers and also local parks and old age homes, and schools.

Clearing litter - you will be assigned to ensure our streets are spotless, this includes removing chewing gum from public transport seats, picking litter up and removing graffiti, unless it's been done by Banksy, then this is a crime to remove as this is art and property of the country.

Pet watchers - you will take care of the pets of the workers during their 12-week annual leave, you will be fully trained and no harm will come to the pet you are entrusted with, if any harm does come to them you will be punished.

Pot hole fillers - you will be trained to be able to fill potholes on demand to ensure our country has no more of these hideous landmarks.

Fan wafters - for all of the countries public transport, you will be required to keep all of the workers cool with fans on their journeys to ensure they arrive at work looking their best.

Bin draggers - you will ensure all of the streets you are assigned to, the bins for the workers are moved from their gardens to the front of the property and back again when it's been emptied, saving the workers a job every week.

Domestic violence street patrollers - you will ensure to step in if at any point you see anyone being bullied or harassed by another human being. You will be trained in Krav Maga and be able to undertake any situation to ensure our streets and homes are safe at all times.

Personal Assistants - to the workers. Your jobs can vary from urine runner to the Doctors to collecting shopping up for them, to chaperoning them home after a night on the tipple, it's at their discretion what jobs you are assigned.

Helpers - you will be assigned to helping the elderly and people with children. If you see someone struggling with shopping or struggling with their pushchairs you will step in and help, you are permanent bag packers and trolley pushers and you will NOT keep that £1 from the trolley.

First aiders - you will be fully trained in first aid. If someone is in an accident and they are made to wait around 3 hours for an ambulance, you will ensure this person is at their most comfortable, by giving them Prosecco on tap, a pillow, a blanket and singing soothing songs to them, to ensure this isn't a horrific wait for them. Some of you will be required to train in ballet, tap and comedy, for their amusement and pleasure.

Superheroes - we can see this job will become a popular one, you will be the ones who walk the streets at night ensuring any crimes taking place are stopped in the first instance. You will be required to undergo training for this role as you may be required to run and be acrobatic. Costumes are not supplied you will have to make your own.

The slappers - you will be required to monitor customer service, to ensure if anyone steps out of line and treats sales assistants horribly, you have the power to slap them, to ensure peace is kept in the community. Abusing this role will result in you being demoted to a worse role.

The friends - you will be required to become friends with the elderly. There will be no elderly person trapped in their homes. You will cook dinner for them and take them out. You will invite them to your home to meet your family for Christmas and you will become their new friend.

On-hand advisors - you will be required to assist those who are unwell and who need someone to talk to at 3am, you will need your phone available 24 hours a day and your role will ensure nobody is alone at times when they need someone. If they require you to attend their homes you will attend to hug, comfort and listen to them.

For the full list of jobs you will be assigned to, please see the leaflet enclosed in this letter to make your decision. *Your income will be based on your job role you will not receive any top ups or benefits. You will be taxed on overtime due to all the benefits you have previously had. You will not receive a bonus and you will only be entitled to 2 weeks annual leave per year which will be paid for by us and is not to be taken at Christmas, school holidays or weekends. You're going to be kept busy as much as possible. When you have proven yourself in 10 years time, you will be moved to the workers section.

The Sick and the Elderly

You don't have to worry about your income, we are going to pay all of your expenditure and ensure you have a little something extra. We appreciate it's not your fault you are unwell or elderly and you will not be punished for this. We are setting up more than enough support groups and investing more money in the healthcare system to ensure you receive the best treatment possible. We don't want you to worry about a single thing. We want you to get well and also to live out your elderly years peacefully, after all you helped us out throughout history and now it's our turn to re-pay this favour. Just relax and we'll do all the hard work, to ensure you see we are working positively to

make your life a lot easier. If you have any questions an advisor who hasn't gone on the cruise will attend your property and put all of your worries at ease.

Any other people *Why are you not in one of the sections, pick one there are no other choices for you!

Throat Jab Thursday

It has finally been announced that the new day of the week is now called 'Throat Jab Thursday'.

This will commence from next week and it's an entire world event.

What does this day consist of I hear you ask? well Throat Jab Thursday is for people that you spend the remaining 6 days of the week being patient and polite too, despite you re-enacting several ways a day on how you will eventually get your own back on them. This day consists of being able to Throat Jab those people that just don't get it, those people that are simple morans that raise your neck hairs daily.

Please find below the details and the rules to this day. Anyone found to be abusing this will suffer severe consequences that entail worse than Throat Jabbing. Be warned.

This system has been put in place to protect those in the world that have been blessed with morals and kindness. Those who don't, will soon discover that they need to somehow find these attributes. Let's join together and hope the world will soon be a better place thanks to this new system. "Happy Throat Jabbing Thursday." *If you or anyone you know are affected by this day from rule breakers, please contact your local authority who will investigate your concerns, If you are found to be misleading the officers you will suffer Monday, Tuesday, Wednesday, Thursday, Friday, Saturday and Sunday Throat Jabbing as punishment.

On this note please don't feel scared to come forward. We are all working together to create positivity and harmony in the world.

Acceptable Throat Jabbing

Those who consistently like their own status's on social network

Those who constantly upload the same selfies

Those who upload the same underwear photos

Those who over do the duck pout on profile
pictures
People that brag about not having to work whilst
you're paying for this privilege for them

Anyone that has had Botox and shows no sadness
when you tell them a family member has passed
away

Anyone that thinks they are a politician when
clearly they're biased to what benefits they're not
receiving

Anyone that uses the word C*** when referring to
sports people, (think you can do better, let's see
you try)

Anyone that blocks you on social networking
despite you doing absolutely nothing to them,
except sleeping with 2 of their boyfriends
previously

Anyone that makes using a public toilet more difficult than it already is (save that S*** for home, no pun intended)

Anyone that drags their child that hard you can visibly see the child's arm coming out of the socket, (make sure to jab this one real hard)

Any driver that mouths the word T*** to you, despite it being your right of way (get out your car, approach them and own that S***)

Anyone that doesn't like "Harry Potter" (self-explanatory)

The drunk friend you spend your entire night out looking after (this can happen every now and again, but not every week)

The jealous friend that grins behind their evil facial expression, they're not really happy for you (get in there, do your thing and then unfriend)

Anyone that rams your ankles with a trolley whilst shopping (I am waiting for the day driving licences for these come in)

Anyone that asks at the checkout if I need a bag when I have a trolley full of groceries

Drivers on their phones

People that spoil your TV show because you have been busy working and it's currently recorded (if you jab hard enough, their vocal cords may be off balance, allowing you a week or two of no spoilers)

Anyone that thinks a reality star is more worthy than an actor

People that eat with their mouths WIDE open

Anyone in the cinema sitting on Pokémon Go!

Anyone that thinks Marvel is just for little kids

Anyone on public transport that allow pregnant women and elderly to stand (take out the entire compartments if you have too)

Anyone in fast food that gets your food order wrong or spells your name wrong on your drink, especially if it is nowhere near your real name

Nose pickers in public

Anyone who thinks taking a baby to the cinema is acceptable just because its rated 12A

Anyone that attends the theatre, cinema, public transport or actually has the nerve to leave the house whilst they have a cough or cold

People that sing over the song you're currently listening to

People being kind to the homeless for the sake of likes on their networking (kind acts don't need a video)

Anyone caught bullying, this includes youngsters being rude to their parents, not to be used on children below the age of 2

Seat kickers, this includes planes, buses, cinema, anywhere that has a seat behind, and someone is angering you

Anyone that sits on their phone saying "Yeah" to you, clearly not listening, whilst your divulging in how bad your day was (examples-you have just been fired, you have been diagnosed with Bi-polar)

Those rich brats in the MAC store that look down on you for purchasing 2 lipsticks whilst they have 1 of every colour in their basket (we all know those ones, and we also know Daddy's paying for it all)

Girls and Boys that pretend to be overly dumb (It may have worked for Marilyn Monroe....you're not Marilyn Monroe)

Anyone behaving as though they are better than everyone else around them

That family member that only contacts you because they want something

*For the full list please see your local authority website or alternatively contact your local authority, but not at 1 minute to 5pm on a Friday, as this will result in you getting Throat Jabbed the following Thursday.

Part five

The hardest thing in life, is being a Vegetarian (and hating Mushrooms)

I don't eat meat, my reasons behind this are as follows:

1) I love animals
2) I love animals on a mutual respect level, where I don't think eating them is very nice
3) I can't swallow meat, when I was younger. I used to constantly chew and chew meat and the idea of having dead flesh in my mouth and stomach made me retch
4) I look at my dog and think I wouldn't eat them so why would I eat other animals
5) I find it repulsing the idea of living off dead flesh
6) It's cruel, the fact we pick and choose when they live and die, and overbreeding is disgusting for the sake of the fast food companies
7) I know I can survive quite happily without meat

8) Dressing a dead cow up with some lettuce and mayonnaise is not mouth-watering too me, I know what it really is, and I see through that s***

9) I feel myself and animals have a connection, that says you're my friends and not my lunch

10) I can go to a farm and I am NOT imagining them on a roast hog, I have a clear conscience

11) I don't like the idea of a mother pig being taken away from her piglet for the sake of someone's bacon sandwich on hangover Sunday

12) It tastes disgusting

13) I am quite happy having a Sunday/Christmas day dinner without that on the side of my plate putting me off my parsnips

14) I don't understand, how anyone that is a big meat eater doesn't feel guilty about the number of animals they have consumed throughout their life

15) How does someone sit picking dead animal flesh out of their teeth and not question what they're doing

16) I don't believe animals were put on this earth for us to eat, that's my opinion not yours

17) I also don't eat fish, it's the same as above, putting it in tins with a dolphin friendly sticker on the side doesn't make it look more appealing

18) I don't like the idea of eating anything that was once alive or had a face

19) Do you have any backstory about that burger, like the time 'Clarence the cow' ran off from the

herd and had the best day of his life...no you don't even think about it, because animals can't talk you assume their completely stupid, so you don't even know the animals life story

20) I have noticed most of my meat loving friends tend to get sick a lot. I am more than happy to be a veggie lover. I also don't judge anyone that loves meat, I wonder why they enjoy it, but I don't hold this decision against them, after all everyone is free to make their own decisions and have their own opinions.

My gripe is the fact that every single menu for a non-meat eater contains mushrooms! Urghhhh mushrooms are simply on par with meat to me. They look creepy, the texture is somewhat furry inside which distresses me. They taste disgusting, just the thought of putting one between my teeth gives me the same experience as a fork being scratched down a blackboard.

My question is, why do all restaurants automatically assume that people that don't eat meat must live off mushrooms?!?!? mushroom quiche, mushroom Ravioli, mushroom Bake, take those god damn things off my Vegetarian pizza before this s*** gets serious, mushroom mushroom mushroom!!! NO PEOPLE! some veggies do NOT like mushrooms!

They like salads, vegetables, cheese, vegetarian substitutes like pies etc, pizza, chinese food, they do not all wake up and start the day with a mushroom omelette and then have a mushroom salad for lunch, to come home after the gym to have a mushroom Smoothie, followed later by mushroom pie and chips, to just before bed having a cup of tea with a mushroom sandwich?!?!?!?!!? We eat more than mushroom, in-fact I detest them, and it would be nice to go to a restaurant and look at the menu and think wow look at all the selection there is and there's no mushroom in sight.

The next time you're in a restaurant look at the Vegetarian options. I can't tell you how difficult it becomes when you have to order 6 sides to make your pretend dinner up, because people are not imaginative enough to understand that non meat eaters would like to have other options than a furry piece of fungi pulled out the ground, get this girl a carrot...... That is all…

Real Friend Vs Pretend Friend

Do I look ok in this?
PF-You look hot! I love it, I wish I was wearing that now!

RF-No, your ass is eating most of it, how is your vagina not screaming out for mercy, it's way too tight for you to wear!

Do you think he likes me?

PF-Definitely he was staring at you all night, I mean proper staring like he was in love or something?

RF-He likes anything with a pulse!

Am I a good friend?

PF-Of course you are, I wouldn't spend so much time with you, if you weren't, don't be silly you're the best!

RF-stop being a t*** and then yeah, you're ok.

Do you think I'm putting weight on?

PF-Whaaaaaaaaaaat! are you crazy, you're way too skinny now!!!! I wish I was slim like you!

RF-Yes, yes you are, and its mainly down to you eating way too much and spending 6 nights a week watching reality shows, get a life and then get skinny again

I can't afford to go out tonight!

PF- You don't need to worry about that, I have us sorted, and lets' face it when do we ever pay for drinks

RF-Get a F***ing job then

I am in agony I hate mother nature!!!!

PF- have you taken anything to help, hot water bottle? I feel your pain babe, I suffer really badly

RF-Do you think that's pain??? Bitch suck it up, like your mother did for the 37 1/2 hours she spent trying to get your fat ass out of her vagina

Do you think I'm needy?

PF-No of course not, sometimes you just need a little reassurance, we all do

RF- you're doing it now, shut up!

Do you think I will be a good mum when I am older?

PF-are you kidding, a mini you, they will be adorable, and you will be amazing at being a mum, you're so caring all the time

RF-Yeah probably, your kid will come in handy going in town when they're 3 years old collecting your vodka, fake nails and spray tan, personal little shopper right there, great parenting and a smart move for you to have a mini slave on hand really

I really love you, you're like the bestest friend anyone could ask for!!!

PF-aww I love you too, let's get a selfie!!!! duck pouts at the ready

RF-F*** off Did you tell Maddison I kissed her boyfriend?

PF-No why would I say something like that, I may have accidentally said something, oh no, I am so sorry, I feel like I have betrayed you, I didn't mean too :(

RF-Yes.......and? you want to suck on someone else's boyfriend's face, then man up and own it!

Part six

Pet Peeves Part One

Slow WIFI connections, I don't care if its free, make it work!

People that like their own status's (please self-gratification or what!)

People that don't flush the toilet

People that spoil the TV show you haven't caught up, because you actually have a job, but they break their necks to spread it all over the internet, give me time!!!

Judgemental people (pot kettle black)

Angry drivers (don't shout at me, it's my right of way)

The drunk person behind me in the queue that smells of urine, and I have too many items and not enough fingers to put one on my nose

People that are too nice

People that smile permanently...weird!

The drunk person that drops his kebab outside my house, and then his stomach lining a few feet down

People that talk very loudly on the train

People that stare at me on the train

People that stare at me in general

People that drag their dogs like their dragging their rubbish outside

Hostile dentists

Doctors that don't listen to you and their entire office has Dalmatian dog pictures everywhere
The person in the takeaway queue that is listening intently to what I am ordering
Silent taxi drivers…awkward
People that sit liking every single person's status and its' all down your news feed
Anyone that participates in "Black Friday"
The security officer at the airport that always tips my entire hand luggage everywhere to search it (no secrets to a woman's handbag anymore, that's ok to leave a month's worth of my Tampax on the top of the pile, wasn't trying to hide them anyway)
People in Customer Service that clearly hate their job
People that don't check missing items on the shelf, because they have a memorised every item in the entire store and know exactly what's in the warehouse
People being extra nice to then hand me a feedback card
Copycats, whatever happened to being original
People that overuse words they know you hate "Moist"
Aggressive people
People that abuse and take for granted, the beauty of the world that is surrounding them
People that show off with their possessions, but we all know your secret......credit!

Questions I ask myself

Where do I fit into this world?

What is my purpose in this world?

Do I contribute to this world in a positive way?

What would people say about me if I were no longer here?

How would someone describe me to someone else?

Am I different to other people in a good way?

Is there something else after this world?

Is this world a test ready for a greater world we can only imagine in dreams?

Where do I go when I am sleeping, I am sure I go somewhere, I always have jet lag when I wake up?

What will I look like as I start to age?

Will I have regrets?

Why can't I let my inner self out and enjoy my life instead of speeding through it?

Am I the kind of person people would miss?

Do I ever inspire anyone?

Am I as funny as I think I am?

Are my impressions good or do people laugh because there bad?

Why can't I stick to eating healthy?

Should I try to stick to eating healthy foods?

Why do we put shampoo on our hair, it's got poo in it?

Is there someone out there for me but I don't even realise it?

Am I going to end up a cat lady despite not ever wanting to own a cat?

What career am I meant to be actually doing?

Does past experience determine future moments?

Will I ever stop selling my unwanted Christmas presents online?

Will my mum ever find out I do this?

Should I get my sister an extra-large present this year, to secure she doesn't out me to my mum for selling presents she has given me?

Is my dog playing hard to get with my affection?

Can the Government watch me through my phone and TV?

Am I memorable?

Will there ever be a cure for Cancer?

Why can't I learn to cook?

Am I too outspoken?

Do great things lie ahead for me?

Will I ever learn to accept my own insecurities and flaws?

Should I tire myself out trying to change them?

If people described me in 3 words what would they be?

Is it ok to feel completely unhappy in the job you're doing for the sake of doing a job?

Am I someone's soul mate?

Is it ok to eat Wotsits (cheese puffs) and Peanut Butter sandwiches without people judging me?

Will I ever be able to clean my tongue without retching?

Will I ever be able to complete "Donkey Kong" without cheating?

Why do I quit smoking to then start again?

Will anyone ever have that moment with me where they lose their breath over the sight of me, in a good way not a shocked way?

Is my mum proud of me?

Are my family proud of me?

Can demons ever be put to bed without medication and therapy?

Does everything happen for a reason?

Will I ever be able to watch "Titanic" without crying?

I wonder where the furthest place in the world is, I will go too?

Is it realistic to have a bucket list because I keep adding too it?

Will all the people around me know how much I love them if I am no longer able to say it?

Is it possible to accept mistakes made in the past and be able to move on from them?

Will I ever tire of the song "She's always a woman" by Billy Joel?

Is my Gym membership a complete waste of time?

Will my fear of tin foil ever leave me?

Will my breasts grow anymore?

Why did I forget to put the bin out yesterday, now I will have 4 weeks of rotting rubbish in my garden?

Will I ever own a car that wasn't born prior to 2000?

Where will the Marvel Franchise be in 10 years-time?

Which do I like more the shower or the bath?

Will I wake up one morning and not know who I am anymore?

Why do I hold on to so much scrapbook memories throughout my life?

Does it ever actually bother me when someone deletes me from social networking sites?

Will there ever come a day I start drinking Diet Coke?

Will I ever learn to stop using the word F***?

Will I ever not get goose bumps and feel emotional at theatre shows?

Does everyone else think things like me, or I am unstable?

Pet Peeves part two

Certain high-end clothes stores that clearly undersize their garments, thanks for making me think I have gone up 2 sizes!

Slugs, I don't want to kill them, I don't want them having a rave at my back door either Worms....they have no face. I don't trust anything without a face

Mushrooms....No explanation needed

The people that smell on the underground, I don't want to be that close, but I don't have an actual choice

Certain fast food outlets that always mess my order up, yeah, I didn't order any of the 3 fries that are currently missing...cheers!

Restaurants blaming their staff are rude because its busy and they are under pressure? acceptable I think not, hire more staff then!

Pop up adverts.... everywhere!!!!!

The local shop that's just sold me "Bonjela" 4 years out of date, yeah, I wanted my gums to corrode anyway

Tin openers

Paper cuts

People moaning about the weather

That person that's always in the gym and it shows

That person on social media that puts "It's snowing" as soon as a flake drop's

Self-service checkouts

Boxing day, I miss Christmas day. It's like the death of Christmas and there is no boxing in it

People that don't mash potatoes enough

Rude people at car boots that send their children to barter an item from £4 down to 50p, do it yourself

People making cups of tea snow white. Where's the god damn tea?

Being told off when you're hysterically laughing, when will people realise it just makes the laugher worse, let it out

Pot smokers in the park, just do it at home you're not actually being that discreet here

People who think they know everything about someone

Rumour spreaders, do you not realise this destroys people's lives

Selfish people

That girl at dinner that exclaims she can eat and eat and eat and just not put any weight on, please choke on your 5th pork chop, please don't bring the bill, she might eat that as well

Dream crushers, those people that batter you down because they are scared you may achieve great things

Friends that don't tell you when you have food in your teeth

The same friends that also don't tell you, you have lipstick on your teeth

Junk mail that gets into your inbox, no thank you I have no desire for a penis enlargement Talking of emails........

Emails I would prefer not to receive

I have a battle constantly daily, with unsubscribing to companies I have never subscribed too, it's frustrating, time consuming, and in all honesty the emails keep on coming despite on several occasions politely requesting I do not receive these emails in future.

The biggest culprits are Penis enlargement-no matter how many times I unsubscribe, this one just keeps coming, no pun intended.

Quickhotsexrightnow-Hmmm again I am unsure why I keep requesting not to receive these, but they continue to come through as quick as it takes for me to unsubscribe to them.

Russian women for me-Vlada wants to talk to me now, I don't think going by her name she wants to talk to me, more like drain my neck and my bank account.

How to get an erection that lasts-Trust me it doesn't work, I haven't ever experienced an erection in my life, despite this company telling me I can. I personally wouldn't recommend this, false advertising if you ask me.

*My biggest fear in life, losing my phone, someone gaining access to my emails and someone thinks I actually use these places!

Part seven

The London Underground system

Have you ever had the pleasure of travelling on the London Underground as a tourist? I have every single time I take a trip down there. I will break down what I have found whilst enduring this painful way of public transport.

1) Hygiene issues-you're going to get up close and personal, most likely with someone who hasn't washed in at least 4 days. Don't expect anything less. You will endure the disgusting mashed up scent of unwashed clothes, with sweat from someone that also doesn't own a toothbrush. There is no getting away from this once your packed in like a sardine. And the worst part when you run to jump in the carriage it's only then you realise the doom you have just cursed on yourself for the next 8 stops. And it's only going to get worse. Because on every single stop you will encounter more sardines, and let's face it would you want to soak yourself in a bath of sardines to relax, I think not. Just hold your breath for as long as you can if your ever unlucky enough to be put in this position. Count down the stops and try not to choke.

2) The silence-unless it's the tourists chattering away in the language they use; you won't very often see the actual people that live in London chattering away. It's like some kind of silence code that is not to be broken. So, if you end up in a carriage that is full of Londoners you may find you don't want to chatter away. The silence is something that just becomes the norm. When you do start talking you may experience a few raised eyebrows as to why you are talking. Shhhhhhhh people from London don't want full blown conversations while travelling home from work, they want silence, they have probably just worked an 18-hour day to afford the home there, you get it?

3) The starer-now most Londoners will happily sit on the tube in silence, some even go to sleep as they have now set a body alarm clock for their chosen destination. It isn't unusual to sit opposite people with their eyes closed, they could be meditating or maybe they just don't want to look at you, you, hideous person. Now the ones with their eyes open are either reading a book or re-reading the banners above your head. But you will experience a starer. That one person who will lock eyes on you, look you up and down, and refuse to blink. The best way to deal with the starer is to act as though they didn't look at you and keep re-reading the banner above their head. If you

continue to stare at them, you are going to lose and it's only going to get hostile. Just look away, don't start chattering to the person you're with, remember the silence code and don't choke from the unwashed person standing over you. The starer will check out what shoes you're wearing and what bags you're carrying, they may be curiously working out who you are and what you do and what planet you have just come from. Just breathe there is only 6 stops of this left.

4) The free rider-It's also not unusual to see the hard-faced ticket inspectors who appear more like bailiffs than friendly ticket inspectors and the job there to do is ensure everyone has paid for the above pleasures. If you don't have a ticket prepare to be outed in front of the entire carriage and believe me the starer is going to marvel in your embarrassment. You will have to explain in front of a silent carriage why you can't afford a ticket but you're on there anyway, where you got on, and

where you intend to get off. Who you are and your personal details, and if this isn't bad enough you will be turfed off at the next stop by the mean looking ticket inspector, so everyone waiting on the platforms will know you're a free rider and you will get more than a hundred eyes on you and no less than 25 tuts! Know that it won't end there, you will be the conversation for the rest of the day "I can't believe someone thinks they can ride the tube for free" and you may even get a status on social networking for now you have become a celebrity in your own right. "just saw someone get thrown off the tube, sneaky"! usually with the laughing emoji.

5) Those who just don't get it-You will occasionally see the man who runs and takes the doors like he is involved in an Olympic event, to only get pie-faced because he gets the front of his foot jammed in the door, or the person that gets the doors shut on them and its left to the remaining sardines to help pull them in. It's clearly dangerous, don't try it, it's embarrassing, and the other sardines are only going to spend the entire journey marvelling at you with their eyes, on whether you have a death wish or your just simply a risk taker.

6) The phone people-there will be one or several people on their phone every now and again, discussing something about their private life and which stop they are at. Now what gets me every time is I get zero signal on the underground, so I am always curious as to which phone network allows them this delight, I am more interested in trying to work this out, rather than the conversation their having, which shouldn't be so loosely discussed on the tube. It makes the other

sardines uncomfortable, not only is their silence being broken, they are forced to endure the rattle of someone who is disgruntled about the party last night. We know this from the make-up you have applied over last night's make up.

7) The angry ones-sometimes, it doesn't happen often, but it does happen. You will come across the angry tube goers and most of the time whilst they are hurling abuse at you while they are running for the tube, you will have no idea on what you did to anger them or what exactly is happening. The best way to deal with this situation is walk very slowly to the platform hoping that by the time you have arrived this angry sardine has already taken the tube. Because if not, they will still be cursing you from the other end of the platform. There appears to be no reasoning with them and it's best not to approach them. Just don't acknowledge how angry they are, there is no point trying to work out why you made them as mad as they are. Play dumb, it could be something as small as you stood in their way and their day is already hell. Just take it on the chin and don't react. If you feel approaching them is the best situation, then ask yourself, (would you take a bone from a lion?) it is pointless just carry on with your day, don't take it personally like I did previously, (I questioned over and over again what I could of done, and if I am a bad person,) because it will eat you away and it's not worth it.

8) Summertime heat-So you didn't' think England would be hot because our summers suck right? wrong, get down on the underground in the summer and your brain will trick you into thinking you accidentally landed in Mexico. It's hot down there, with all the sardines there isn't much oxygen. Take water and don't go on the undergrounds when you have raided all the shops on Oxford street you will regret it. Your body will produce sweat from glands presently unknown about, and let's face it, do you really want to be put in the league of sweaty and unwashed? Keep cool and take water with you and brush your teeth just for courtesy of the others around you.

9) Platform etiquette-get out of the fricking way. Don't stand there like a deer in the headlights. Keep away from the ledge on the platform, it's dangerous and I am pretty sure you don't want the highlight of your trip to be you ended up in front of a train. There is a reason they have "Stand clear of the platform signs". Don't block pathways, find somewhere you can stand out of the way with your ten suitcases, and if you refuse to move you will encounter the angry one.

10) The escalators from hell-depending on where you stop at you will nearly always encounter the escalators. Now the golden rule is if you don't

want to walk them, stand to the right. Leave a gap for those who are running late and want to hurdle up the stairs. There are signs everywhere that inform you to move to the right. If you break this rule, then you will have to deal with a lot of sardines behind you hurling abuse. If you want to become a sardine sandwich then stay on the left, but it is always advised to just remember the right side is the safe side, you are in your comfort zone by following the rules.

11) Getting out of the ticket doors-just as a precaution, if you have a lot of shopping bags then I would advise you go through the ticket gate for the wheelchairs and pushchairs. Don't be rude and barge in front of someone who clearly is in a wheelchair, and you don't need to put a fake limp on, no one is handing out Oscars in the underground. But the other ticket doors are like a Venus flytrap, as soon as you have put your ticket in, move move move!!!!!

I have previously been trapped in these doors and it's more than embarrassing having to get told off by the angry ticket woman who is related to the angry person on the tube you just encountered. She has no sympathy for you, and she is probably sick to death of seeing people just like you, who think you have all the time in the world to stroll freely through this gate. Wrong, get your ass moving.

London is fast paced, if you can't hack fast paced go and visit a desert island instead.

Ticket in, move!

Happy exploring the capital..........

How to deal with a broken heart

Don't take it personally. It's not you, sometimes it's just not meant to be.

You may not see through the tears right now and the hurt you feel from your head and your heart, but in a matter of time, you will be able to see more clearly.

Sometimes people just aren't compatible, and they're not meant to be.

There is someone out there that will love you like the Princess/Prince you deserve to be treated like.

Someone's heart is longing to find you, and when the puzzle pieces fall into place you will be glad your heart was broken, because if it wasn't, you would never have found the divine love that is out there waiting for you to come and seek it.

Pick yourself up off the floor and wipe those tears away from your beautiful face. Do not beat yourself up, you were good enough for them, they were not good enough for you.

Hold my hand and I will walk with you through life until you find the one that makes you feel complete.

Do not turn to alcohol, or social networking, you will not find any solace in these things.

Fix yourself day by day and grow back into the beautiful person you are.

Tubs of ice-cream can help to numb your heart and sometimes your brain, but again this is only a quick fix.

You may not feel it now and your heart is in pain, but when you find yourself again you will be surprised to learn how strong this experience has made you.

Do not think this is the end, for it is only the beginning.

It's ok to put yourself through romantic films and feel sad, but only for a short time, you can't wallow in self-pity for long periods of time, you are stronger than this.

Cry it out and build yourself back up. Focus on you, but don't change you! You have no reason to change.

The person that will fall completely and madly in love with you, will fall for you, not the person you change to be. If someone tries to change you, walk away. For you are you and someone great will see this. Don't ever try to be someone you are not, for you will spend your entire life unhappy and trapped in a lie.

Surround yourself with people that love you. It may not be the same kind of love, but it's love.

They will help you, sometimes in silent ways, they will help you mend your broken parts and make you see what a wonderful person you really are. You need this gentle reminder.

Negative thoughts need to be pushed away, do not allow them to take over your feelings. Remind yourself the reasons why you have a broken heart. Do not keep replaying the what if's, they won't help you. Do not look back, looking back is not moving forward. It's easy to get back together, but there was a reason it didn't work the first, second and third times. Your heart is worth more than a constant replay of sadness.

Love yourself, respect yourself and enjoy finding the one who will marvel at you as a person. That person that will love every inch of you inside and out. That person who will love the things that you so often to hide from shamefulness.

Take time to have some duvet days, its ok. No-one expects you to just switch off.

Grieving is one of the hardest things you will ever have to do, whether the person is here or now departed. But duvet days are a temporary fix, it is not ok to do this long term, how will you ever stand strong again if you are laying down every-day.

You are the one who will need to fight through all of these overwhelming feelings. You may feel alone, but you are not. Think it over and then realise sometimes situations can be out of your control. Sometimes life has a bigger plan for you. You are destined for a bigger greatness than what you feel now.

You will never be alone in the world. There are always people you can turn to and the chances are, they also felt this at some point in their life, look at them, they survived to tell the tale.

And yes, you're as strong and as brave as them, keep telling yourself this over and over again. It will get easier, maybe not today, but tomorrow is a new day.

Trust me, I have been there, and I have learned a hard lesson. It gets easier the more times it happens. You can survive, you will be ok, you will go on to greater things and when you find your prince/princess, you will realise that all of the ones before were merely frogs, and we all know the fairy tale of kissing the frog to find your prince/ princess.

It's not going to be easy, you will feel low and helpless, but please remember this may feel overwhelming and uncontrollable right at this moment, but I promise you it won't always feel this way, and if you believe it was meant to be with that person, then life will bring them back around again and fate will give you both a helping hand.

Do not dismiss anything and don't think everything is always forever, life has a funny way of surprising you, and remember, it will be worth all of the heartache to find the greatest love of all, nothing spectacular will come easily in this life, the best things are worth all of the pain and heartache, you just need to realise you will have to fight for them and all of the heartache you have felt will just become stored in your memories and the pain will feel like a million life time's away..... I promise.

My dog hates me! The personality of a Shar-Pei

I honestly feel as though my dog hates me.

She's always pleased to see me when I come home from wherever I have been, but I see this sinister motive in her eyes, it isn't a greeting, it's more a hostile invisible threat. Almost as though she is glad, I am back for her to torture me. Her real-life toy is back for her to play with.

Although to date she hasn't played with toys, her favourite past time is to steal coat hangers and chew them apart, I'm debating on whether she is secretly clever enough to make something from these that could potentially pick locks. She once took a hanger for trousers and bit into it so hard she got her lip stuck between the teeth on it, the whine was enough to alert the national service, and her face when I took the teeth off her lip and I tried to console her was "YOU did this to me".

I don't get lay ins. Regardless if I go to bed at 10pm or 6am, she will not allow me to have any form of lay in. She will spend most of the morning barking at every single thing in the house and anyone that comes within 10 feet of the house. She has lost several teeth from biting the letterbox as she has some kind of fixation that the postman is the devil and he is posting a letter that declares I have to hand over my soul to him.

Every time a letter is posted she goes into robot mode to destroy this letter; this letter is the enemy. This letter is her arch enemy and because the postman has the absolute brashness to put this through our door he too is her enemy. She spends hours in the week watching him out of our windows and anyone that has a similar coloured jacket must also be destroyed. For the only person who shall be taking my soul is my dog herself. I often arise to letters covered in blood, from her biting the now metal letter box cover I have had installed. I have mixed emotions receiving good news letters covered in blood it's almost as though the letter becomes a secret threat.
I am seriously considering if there is another option such as a box on the wall outside to save this noise and frustration and to preserve at least 3

of her teeth. I am just worried her frustration may take my door down next.

I have seen her in action many a time and she fights to the death, there is no separating her from this letter box, I have tried unsuccessfully on several days to only receive a non-friendly warning not to interfere again. It's similar to watching the "Next" sale shoppers at 5am on boxing day, they are there to fight to the death regardless of who crosses their paths, an even closer example would be "Black Friday" you just don't take the same item someone else is reaching for, unless you want to end up on the floor with potentially a 55" TV thrown on you, all for the sake of some reduced item that could save you 20% on and this is how my dog is with our letterbox, don't touch her, don't touch it, just sit and watch it unfold 6 days a week, thank heavens the post doesn't come on a Sunday.

But then again, she makes up for this on a Thursday when the rubbish collectors arrive. So, I guess you could say it's pretty much a full-time thing. I feel as though contagion has somewhat taken over her when she catches the glimpse of the rubbish collectors. There is red eye and frothing at the mouth. But I have no prescription for this disease to give her.

The man who comes along quite happily to remove the stench rotting rubbish that has been sitting stagnant in the bin for 2 weeks. This man is doing me a favour he is ridding my garden of the pesky rotten smell of decomposing food. But my dog does not see this. In my experience my dog sees this as "He must be destroyed" for he is daring to approach our house and touch our stuff. She also has some sort of grudge against the bin once it's dragged back into the garden, almost as though the bin has gone off with the bin man and betrayed her trust. I find all of this behaviour somewhat strange and unsettling.

My dog is also very calculated, she is very good at pretending to be asleep. I sneakily step over her to approach the kitchen to obtain some sort of snack late at night, to come back in and see her smug face licking my entire cup of tea, regardless of how hot or cold this drink is, this will also consist of orange juice, fizzy drinks, you name it, I have learnt NEVER to leave alcohol anywhere around her through past experience, which I would not care to go through again. I never thought I would experience a drunk dogs bark, its similar to a horn dying, slowly running out of life or a dog that's so hungover the next day, they can't even be bothered to attempt to go towards the back door for fresh air, instead she just casually vomits all over the floor and then looks up at me with what I could only imagine are the words "YOU did this to me"

It's the same with food, are you getting the picture?. She looks at me with disgust if I light a cigarette for of course she is a non-smoker, and she makes no shyness of letting me know exactly what she is thinking without words. Her flatulence is at its greatest when I am smoking, which I have decrypted into she would rather smell the gas harbouring inside her own body than to allow the smell of smoke anywhere near her exceptional nostrils. I often wonder if she plans to release this whilst I am eating as again, this appears to be some sort of pattern, I have often pushed my dinner to one side for fear of opening my mouth and inhaling the gas, its more deadly than Sarin gas and I would rather much keep my nervous system intact.

I find the scariest moments are when I wake in the middle of the night to see her standing staring over me, I feel it's her breath that actually stirred me to wake in the first place, which is comparable to the bottom of my 2 week old rubbish bin. I do a sudden jump for no matter how many times she does this, it's still as scary as the first time. I sit bleary eyed while she slowly walks off and goes to the bottom of my bed, which by the way is now hers. There is an intense atmosphere while I await that last glare off her before she turns her back to me. I am in no position to request she moves. She secured this spot seven and a half years ago and she has no plans of ever being evicted. I think I am her lodger in this bed.

I have tried to shut her out my room, but she spends all night torturing my ears by licking the bedroom door, and there is only so much of that I can take, it feels worse than a fork on a frying pan, it somewhat drills my ears, so I give in and let her show me who owns this house. Also, I can't keep re-painting the door, sooner or later the door will completely disintegrate from the deadly salvia that appears from her chunky lip flaps during this licking ritual.

The other scary moment is when I use the toilet, in which I have a habit of leaving the door open, I am not always open to the idea that whatever germs arise from an open toilet lid are going to be completely confined in the room with me, and I feel more at ease leaving the door open, so the germs can escape away from me. However, I have found that my dog has some sort of weird obsession with watching me while I use the toilet. It's an eerie feeling, like I know someone is watching me and I turn my head slowly to see her hunched on all fours with her head bowed down and her eyes looking at me in utter disgust. It's a situation I will never get used too. Yes, I could close the bathroom door but then I will have the germs to deal with rather than her piercing stare and I haven't figured out which one is worse.

She has taken over my home that much, when visitors arrive its almost watching the scene play out that they are her guests and I am the dog in the background being told to sit. I watch this replay over and over again, and even now my visitors spend more time greeting her than me. I secretly feel they all know the power she holds and to stay in her good books she is the host who will receive the fuss and greetings. I have accepted this.

The most confusing part of our relationship is, I hinder her with only good feelings. I walk her on my dinner breaks, I feed her well, she is loved and safe, she is clean and warm and well looked after. I try to fuss her, but I have realised she has some sort of anxiety so when I am fussing her, to her it's as though I have an alternative motive and she jumps away from me as though I am carrying the plague. I have tried to gently show her affection but again despite being in a coma, I am the bad person for awaking her and she moves across the room. Looking at me with absolute disgrace that I dare approach and touch such royalty. I try to show her subtle kindness by trying to play ball with her, or bite the rag, but she looks as me as though she is thinking "Are you kidding peasant you chew the rag, I wouldn't fetch that ball if my life depended on it" and play fights with her turn into aggression, she starts off friendly biting and it turns into a full blown fight to the death, so again I walk away for I feel she has an enormous amount of anger towards me.

I can't really understand where this anger comes from. I do however achieve payback on certain times, like Christmas when I dress her as Rudolph, you can tell her facial expression is saying "YOU did this to me" and then I plaster her photo all over social networking sites. Sometimes I purposely eat her favourite kind of food in front of her without sparing her any scraps, just to establish who the real boss is in this house and I constantly sing musicals to her on a loop so she is a part of the music I am listening to in my ears. I always give her more bubbles than bath when it's cleaning time, I take her to the vets for vaccinations and nail cutting sessions, but I am still baffled as to why she could possibly dislike me and if you haven't gathered.....it's not just a dislike, I think she actually............she hates me!

Oh, the personality of a Shar Pei, there is nothing quite like it.

Questions Unanswered

If the sun shined 24 hours a day would I get fed up of feeling warm all the time?

If I could reach up and touch a star and make a wish, would I have enough wishes for all those stars?

If I could find the end of a rainbow would I want to?

When it snows why isn't there enough to roll around in it?

Why do I enjoy sleeping, but never go to bed early?

How come the bubbles never stay in my bath?

How come the stupidest things make me laugh, but jokes don't?

Why do I always say I hate shopping, when I get home, but then I do it again the next week?

What defines a great song? The lyrics or the tune?

Why are Pringles so addictive, what do they put in them?

If I travelled the world would I be content, or would I go around again?

Why am I obsessed with buying things I don't need?

Does anyone want to work?

Does everyone have the same fears in life?

Why do people enjoy violence?

Why can't dogs talk?

If we can put a man on the moon, how come we can't cure cancer?

How come all swear words aren't in the dictionary, everyone uses these words?

Do you think the Government picks each week's lottery winners?

How would life be without cinema or music?

Who came up with the name tiddly winks for a game?

Why don't people have red or purple eyes?

What's more romantic watching the sun rise or staring at the stars?

How come we have a Sunday dinner but no Thursday dinner?

How come I could sit here all-day asking questions, but still not realise the answers or just google them? And how come you can ask a question with a question?

43 Things I can't live without (Not listed in importance level)

Oxygen

Family

Friends

Loyalty

Dreams

Hope

Chocolate

Films, (Cinema or at home) Books TV

My phone

Wotsits (cheese puffs) and Peanut Butter
Sandwiches (it's my entire diet)

Velvet Teddy Lipstick

Eyeliner

Music

Theatre

Motivation

My dog

Vitamin tablets

Holidays

Carrot Cake

Key lime Pie

Pyjamas

Toilet roll

Toothpaste

A toothpick or several

Love

Bread

Sunglasses

Trees

Stars

Rain

Reflexology

Laughter

The occasional rainbow

A daily newspaper

Snow

The smell when its finished raining (Petrichor)

The smell when the grass has been cut (Trauma, I feel very bad the grass is trying to save itself from the injury just been caused) Ok maybe I could live without the Trauma smell as that's got to me!

A Doctor occasionally, (if all else fails, the internet will give me the worst possible outcome for my illness)

Yorkshire Puddings

35 things I don't need in my life (In no particular order of high importance)

Negativity

Fake friends

Stress

Stupid advice

A stalker

Any of the top diseases that google suggest I have
when I am researching Flu symptoms

Friends online I have never met before and they
live 5000 miles away

Heatstroke

Meat

Mushrooms

An alarm clock

A flashy car

A wardrobe full of flashy clothes

Acceptance

A high earning promotion

The flu from the person behind me at the cash
machine that has just sneezed on my back

High strung and a bit wild

Penny J Bond

A Mortgage

Debt

My own self-doubts

Bad memories that won't leave me alone

Hurtful words

Regrets

Swimming in the sea

Tinfoil

Worms

Death

Spots

Hangovers

Heartache

Low self esteem

Toothache

High strung and a bit wild

Penny J Bond

Being sick and unwell

Violence

Parking Tickets

No signal

Part eight

The Dark Tunnel

You find yourself in a tunnel, it's dark, it's cold, it's wet, it's the loneliest place to be.
There is the smallest light, which is a million miles from where you stand, it's the only thing you can see in the pitch blackness of your surroundings.
Your shoes are soaking, you're standing in water, the icy cold-water creeps up around your ankles and it's uncomfortable.

You smell nothing but the dampness around you. You're there for so long that the coldness takes over you, your teeth have been chattering for so long you are worried they will break, everything angers you, you're worn down from your teeth to your inner soul, your spirit feels weak like it's fading away.

You walk and walk for days, for weeks, for months, there is no real concept of life or of time. Food is no longer a necessity, everything that you would do on a normal day is no longer a necessity to you, you're mentally exhausted, you overthink how you got into this tunnel in the first place, it's all your mind can focus on, but you have two choices right now, you can keep walking to that distant light, as it's the hope of getting out of this place or you can slump into the icy water, close your eyes, curl yourself up into a ball and do nothing.

Giving in always seems like an easy option when you're this tired. But don't.

Occasionally lanterns light up out of nowhere like someone hits a thousand switches on for you, but you notice that they don't stay on for long. They come and go, and it doesn't feel long enough. It's all in the blink of an eye and it blinds you momentarily. You're delirious, you have no idea how long you have been in here, your body has gone into cruise control and you're just walking, you're so tired, when will this end.

The one thing you know is you don't ever want to feel like this again, but you didn't cause this, you didn't voluntarily walk into the tunnel you were put there, and it's only you that can get yourself out of it. It's hard, it's one of the hardest challenges you will ever have to face, mentally and physically.

You hear voices "keep going" and you question is this real, did you hear that or was your mind playing tricks on you. It's hard to know what's real and what's not when you're this tired, and you feel this sad. It's a sadness like no other, it lives inside of you, manifests itself and takes over who you really are. You don't want to feel like this, but the environment and the manifestation won't allow anything else. It swallowed you up so quickly you didn't have time to react. You're just sadness walking along.

Sometimes you sit and rest, your mind is at its highest during this time and it's at this point that you break down, it's normal, you're exhausted, it's ok to cry. When you do you sob uncontrollably, like you won't ever be able to stop the tears, you question is the water you're treading all of your tears, you feel so alone, this world is so big you wonder how you ended up in a tunnel all alone with not a single soul.

You can't recall how anything other than damp smells, and you have forgotten how your inner soul lights up to the aroma of an autumn day, when the leaves drop slowly by your face and you inhale them as they pass. Every now and then those voices let you know "you're not alone" but it gets muffled in between the overwhelming pain and tiredness and the voices are only distant, sometimes you don't even hear them, it's like the icy water around your feet you're used to it now, you can't remember a time when you were warm

and dry and you felt calm and safe, you have
forgotten about how the sun used to make you feel
all warm and happy from the inside out and you
start to question that light at the end on whether it
is really there or is it just a trick, it's easy to think
you won't make it to the end and that your too
broken now to reach that far.

Don't listen to this thought. My love, you're not
alone I can promise you this. Although you are in a
dark place, and it's cold and I can't take you out of
this tunnel I am here, you just can't see me. Please
wipe your eyes and remember how strong you are.
That pain will fade eventually, but for now this is a
process you need to fight, and it's hard to fight
battles alone, but that light is there for a reason, it's
your way forward, and the more you push through,
the closer you are getting to ending this pain.

Listen to those around you, those voices are the
ones that love you and want to remind you you're
doing great, we all know it's hard, we are all here,
don't let your mind block us out, open your ears if
only for a second. Stand up and battle on, it will be
worth it in the end.

When you get to the end of the tunnel you will be
stronger than you were before you got put here.
You may always have some sadness inside of you
when you get out, but it will be enough for you to

control, it won't be as overwhelming as it is right now at this second.

If I could switch places with you, I would take you out of that tunnel and put myself in it. But this is not my challenge to face, and those lanterns are us my love, all the people that will always be there for you, we are trying to help you fight your battle by showing you the light that is awaiting, sometimes the lanterns go out because we are all in tunnels of our own, but we will always come back to make sure you're ok, now pick up your pace, shake off those thoughts and focus on how much you are loved and how you are determined to get out of this place.

I have been in that tunnel more than once, and the harder the sadness, the harder the tunnel is, but if I can do it, you can do it. I will try to light my lantern more for you, because I know you need it right now, so I will pave the way and help you as much as I can, because you are so important to me and I love you and when you're out of this place, I hope if I get lost in that tunnel again you will help me.

Now come there is a whole world awaiting, the sun is shining, and the autumn leaves are hanging on for you, so take a deep breath, pick up your pace and follow my lantern.

A Promise is Forever

He shuffles his small feet slowly from side to side.
His neck stretched to the right as his tired blue
eyes look around the corner and past the heads of
the younger generation, who are rushing from their
hectic day at work past him.

He holds his overworked hands together as they
slowly move up and down, caused by the
excitement that awaits him. The younger
generation storm through without a glance up or a
care in the world, they don't see people, now their
eyes are all glued to their phones, tapping from one
social networking site to the other, he doesn't
understand it all, technology passed him by and he
felt too old to care about learning about it all, and
before long the entrance to the station is once
again empty, but only for a short time because the
next train is due in any minute now.

He wipes the little amount of hair he has to the
side, this used to be his famous signature in the
1950s, this is how he won her over, with the
utmost care and pride he took in his appearance.
He shuffles once again, maybe it's the excitement
or it could be the cold winter day that surrounds
him and every train that shoots through the station
leaves a chilling freeze behind it.

Today he isn't wearing his proper winter coat, if she was here, she would tell him the jacket he has chosen isn't suitable for this weather. She would have made him put his scarf on, his hat and of course his gloves because she knows that he needs to keep himself warm. She always looks after him.

His eyes avert to the arrivals board, but he struggles to see the board as clearly as he could years ago, his eyes have worked tirelessly for over eighty years, he tries to figure it out but wants to make sure, so he shuffles over to the lady at the ticket counter and asks her when the train he is waiting for will be due in.

He is polite, a gentleman, a man raised to know what manners are, he knows they cost nothing, he comes from a generation where he always opened doors and pulled out chairs for all women, not only his wife but also his mother.

He has his information and he shuffles back to the spot he just left, this is his spot, because this is where he always waits and she will see him straight away when she gets off the train, like an old dog he has the same routine and he won't break it.

Time passes him as he stands still, except for the occasional shuffle of his feet and hands, but this is to keep his blood circulating, he is cold, he has waited here a while, because he thought he had the time right for when her train would arrive, he won't let the cold bother him, the sight of her beautiful face will soon warm his heart up, and before long the younger generation are bustling through the station again, they are all on a mission faster than ever, somewhere to go, someone to see, so much to fit into their busy lives, it's hard for him he doesn't want to miss her, but he also doesn't want to be under the stampede, he shuffles with agitation and as quick as clicking like on a social networking site all of the people disappear like they were never there.

He checks his watch, the watch he has owned for twenty years, she got him it as a gift and as he looks at it, he reminds himself that he is from a generation that fixed anything that was broken, they didn't replace it, that's why he's kept the watch all this time this and the fact it was a present from her, his wife.

His wife for sixty-two years, childhood sweethearts and best friends. He wouldn't ever dream of replacing something his wife bought for him it's far too precious, it means something, it's a memory, it's irreplaceable.

When he arrived at the station it was a clear light sky and now within the blink of an eye it's a dark shade of evening. The sky changed as quickly as his life passed him by, and although his body shows all the signs of hard work and all the trials and tribulations of human life, he still has a fire inside him despite his body wanting to give up. This fire is her. He can't wait to see her beautiful face and her beautiful eyes, that haven't once changed in the seventy-one years he has known her, they have always been the same, adoring and kind.

The seasons could change outside and he wouldn't leave, not until she's here, he has always waited here when she goes off shopping in the town a few miles down the road, he's always met her and he's always waited for her, that was his wedding vow, to always be there for her and he displayed it the whole sixty-two years they were married he won't let her down now.

The young ticket lady comes over to him to ask him what train he is waiting for again, she's noticed his shuffling and how cold he looks, she knows he has been here a lot longer than the other people who wait to collect their loved ones and she has a look of being concerned for him. She invites him into conversation with her, so she can learn who is waiting for and when they are due in. He tells her about his beautiful wife and how she goes shopping in the local town and that he waits to meet her every single time she goes, he tells her how long they have been married and how they met as childhood friends and how the very first time his eyes laid upon her, he knew he wanted to wake up to her kind eyes every day and how he wanted his children to have those same beautiful eyes. He tells her about the watch he hasn't taken off for twenty years because it's a part of her and he has worn it since the moment she gave him it. She even had it engraved so it's got their initials on it. And it's during this trip down memory lane where he shares all his wonderful memories with his wife, that his mind also invites him into memories he might not want to remember, and with that his mind awakens.

His tired eyes avert to the arrivals board and as he stretches his neck to the right once more, he catches the night sky outside, he turns and looks back at the young lady from the ticket counter and it's at this moment that his heart sinks into his feet. He apologises to the ticket lady and turns to leave.

The ticket lady doesn't need an explanation for his behaviour, she knows his face, everyone at the station does and she also knows he has been coming to the station for years waiting for his beautiful wife, who stopped coming back when she passed away nine years earlier, no one tells him because he promised her in their wedding vows that he would always be there for her and even though his mind thinks she will step off the train, his heart truly believes he will see her again……

Part nine

Customer Service

Working in a customer faced job means you are basically a donkey at a piñata party!

The chatters-this one is the one that seems to just come in for a good old chin wag. They don't necessarily want to purchase anything from you, they just come in to tell you about their day. It could be the recent hospital visit they went too, the family member that is coming to visit or even the dreaded conversation about their cat dying. They aren't contributing to your company in terms of money but remember one thing, they come in to talk to you, because they feel they can and remember they may not have anyone else to talk too, so see this as a compliment. You might find them annoying as they are taking up your time, but to them you are a friend.

The quiet one-this one comes in but never says anything to you, sometimes not even a thank you after the service you give them. You personally think they are rude and impolite. Look at it a different way, it could have been a huge struggle for them to come in and even be around people, try not to see them as rude and don't treat them any differently. Just be you, be polite and be aware they may just be battling their own demons and your work place could be an uphill struggle for them, look at it that they are pushing themselves and most likely don't mean to be rude to you by not speaking, they are just focusing on getting through this alone.

The angry ones-every-one has to deal with these characters, you dread it when they walk through the door, you know they are going to be difficult, because there has never been a single time in the four years you have worked there that they have been any different towards you. Your blood starts boiling, and you know you have either a complaint coming your way or an extremely hostile situation to deal with. What you're missing is, they are probably like this to every human being they come into contact with, it isn't you, it's them. They could have had the worst life possible and the anger is just them now, try to think about what they have been through to make them this way. Imagine the worst things that could happen to you and multiply it by one hundred, how would you behave, would you be a care-free happy human being singing along with the birds and dancing around the streets, probably not. Just take a breath it's going to be difficult but give them the same service you would anyone else and do not take it personally.

Life can be cruel sometimes, maybe it's been really cruel to this person.

The jolly ones-we all love these, those happy people that come in and brighten up our day, hallelujah to these ones, they make our day so much better, appreciate them, it must be difficult to stay so positive and happy every second of the day, treat them well as they do you.

The strugglers-these can come across as awkward, they make mistakes they are nervous and unsure what they are asking for. Be patient, they are trying. They could be dealing with lots of issues right now, and something that comes across as simple to you could be a huge deal for them to do. Take your time and make them feel comfortable, they can take their time, don't rush them it will make it more difficult for them, and don't ever mock them, give them credit they are really trying.

The elderly-they are older than you, their bodies don't work at the same pace as a youngster, don't rush them, let them take their time, they are not doing anything wrong, You always get people behind them in the queue tutting and tapping their foot because they want to grab that Starbucks on their way to work but they won't have time because the old person in-front is stealing their precious time. Tough luck, serve this person at their pace, the person who is tapping their foot is doing this because they have already had more than enough of a coffee fix this morning and that extra Starbucks will just have them bouncing off the ceiling, your actually doing them a favour depriving them of any more caffeine. Remember the elderly can't push themselves to run around like youngsters do, give them credit it's not their fault its life. Treat them with respect, offer to help them if you see them struggling, open the door for them, you're going to be this person at some point in your life and then you will regret not giving them some extra time. Imagine everyone's brain is like a completed Rubik's cube, but as you get older the colours start getting shuffled about so your no longer complete, well think of this when serving the elderly sometimes their minds get confused, they can't help it, the colours may no longer be aligned, be patient.

The mouthy kids-everyone gets these, the smart arses that show off in-front of their friends, don't spend time complaining about the younger generation to your colleague, just remember when you was their age and how being cheeky was in your blood, they don't mean anything personal to you, it's just a kid thing. How-ever there are certain rules to this, if they are completely disrespectful then revert to company policy or overcharge them at least this way they will have less money to spend on alcohol and potentially drugs, you will be doing them a favour.

The mixed ones-these ones can come in one day and can be so happy and friendly and then the next time they completely blank you, it's not you, it's something that's happened to them, you can't take everything so personally or you will never survive in the game of customer service, don't let it change your perception on them, sometimes people can't hide their emotions, just go with the flow and treat them the same as you always would.

Working in an office

Typical stereotypes

Drunk person - that is still inebriated when they come arrive in the morning, they could potentially have a drink problem, but the smell of them doesn't hide this secret, or they just love a good tipple after work, don't be too judging.

The office tart - that person who after one drink deems it necessary to get up to some funny business with anyone and everyone that works in the same room.

The ass sniffer - these are everywhere, usually found up the managers crack, it's surprising the manager can do any work with someone hanging from their ass all day.

The informer - you know that one person or several who cannot wait, in fact they wait and spend their days trying to suss out something someone else may have done wrong, so they can get that person into deep s***, which allows a breather for the informer who does no work anyway.

The quiet person - who after working in the same room as you for 3 years you just realise they also work there?

The know it all - who has to interrupt every single person, every single second of the day with all that wise information they think they know.

The optimistic - that annoying person that always has a smile on their face even when every dreadful thing possible is being thrown in their face, what makes them annoying is when you complain there is no milk in the fridge you look like a complete b****, because the optimistic can keep a smile no matter what.

Part ten

New Shoes

A new pair of shoes always makes your inner self more confident. You walk along with your dazzling shoes hoping everyone will look them over, after all they are your new babies, they're there to be looked at.

They are so beautifully finished, every stitch is perfectly aligned, they're polished so perfectly you can see your face in them, and they have that no-one has ever worn these smell.

You take your shoe off endless times and inhale that perfect newness. You slide them on like Cinderella and her glass slipper and it doesn't matter that they hurt, because beauty is pain, right?

You will master walking in them despite the crippling pain and at the end of the day your feet will deserve some rest time, from the constant battering it has received from the 12 miles you have completed today. You tell yourself when you stare at the new blister thats formed today it was so worth it. Because they may be a tiny bit too small, but the cost of a bargain is something you can't pass on.

A few weeks after this begins to wear off, the excitement is over, and you can no longer see your face in them, they are smeared and smudged. You now have every-day life splattered all over your feet. The heel is starting to look worn, no-one will look at these now and be impressed with their dazzling appearance because they are no longer new, and over time they start to look more and more worn out, stitches no longer aligned, the material is all stretched out, the insides are coming apart and the aroma has faded to a smell you don't want to inhale.

The pain is no longer worth it. And then along with all your other shoes they are no longer placed neatly on your shelf like an award, they are now thrown in the bottom of your wardrobe along with all your other torn up shoes in a pile that resembles the shoe graveyard.

There is nothing special about these shoes, there was when you first got them, but you were tricked by the look of them, how attractive they were, how perfect looking they were, you didn't look past that, you didn't consider how comfortable they would be or how long they would last, you just saw a beautiful image and you ran away with it and it was only ever going to be temporary, and before long your already window shopping for your next new pair. Look at all those shoes piled up in the graveyard, and now compare them to relationships.

How many partners have you had where physical attraction drew you in, the look of them, the smell of them, how perfect you looked on their arm, how everyone looked at you, and then look at how many of those relationships didn't last because the other person changed, they got lazy, they grew older and before long they looked nothing like they did when you first decided to get them.

If you had of looked for someone that didn't automatically just catch your eye, you could have ended up with a pair of shoes that was still attractive but the best part about them was how comfortable they made you feel, and it was this quality that made everything else so good, and it was ok for you both to change because you are not just together because you both look good, but because you make each other feel good.

There are no painful moments, no blisters at the end of the day and no regrets on purchasing them. This is the relationship that won't get thrown at the bottom of your wardrobe, this is the relationship that will withstand the test of time, because that partner you picked will last for years.

Find a pair of shoes that fits you perfectly.

That Girl

To the girl who pretends to like me
You know your face, the one you've got
The one that you think, makes you hot
It's hard for you to smile at me
Your hatred this, I clearly see
I can't recall a single time; I did something bad to you
So why the hate you direct at me?
It isn't something new I see you stare and whisper with people, directly at my face
One of these days I will approach you, with an extra-large can of mace
You're one of those girls, who hates on other girls for no reason at all
You have no motive and no justification, to actually sit and name call
Did I get attention from someone, perhaps looked good one day?
And now the attention from you, has all been taken away
Why don't you speak to me and put your issues to bed?

Instead of treating me, like you wish I was dead
I would act like you're not actually there
But today you have last night's vomit stuck in your
hair
Due to this it's hard to not notice you stink
The smells burning my eyes and making me blink
I heard you had fun with 2 blokes last night
This is clear to the office, you look a right sight
Before judging others take a look in that glass
You are the opposite of a picture of class
That mean girl who's mood swings flickers
Should I tell you, your skirt is tucked in your
knickers?

A three course meal

It's in the pit of your stomach, it's always there just
silently waiting to be triggered by the smallest
comment or insult.

One minute you're calm feeling content and then,
it's like a storm, it comes out of nowhere, you
shock yourself, you're puzzled, you didn't feel it
creep up, you just know it's now there, in full
explosive reaction.

You feel foolish for not being able to control it,
you regret words you speak, you feel guilt, on top
of frustration, because once again your mouth and

your mind took over, it all came from the pit of your stomach.

The scary part is you know it will always be there, nothing cures it. Nothing fixes it, and although you tell yourself it will be more manageable in future, you are always wrong.

You find yourself repeating the same situations over and over, having to apologise for your outburst and the hurtful words you spoke. You didn't even have chance to think about those words that rolled off your tongue, they just slipped out. And you are sorry, of course you are sorry.

It's all your fault. You blame yourself for the person you are, hurtful.

The pit of your stomach is full of anger, full of sadness, full of regret, full of disappointment. It's the biggest meal you ate in your life and there was no digesting it that is the problem. How do you digest emotion?

It started in your childhood, when you were given the starter to this meal, a starter that consisted of grief, pain, fear, disappointment. It continued into your teenage years, where you were served the main course of regret and sadness and then when you were an adult you were dished up an even bigger dessert. A dessert of the starter and main courses constantly repeating on you. It's not the sweet dish you're thinking of, it's sour, a dessert you wouldn't order at a restaurant. You were force fed this meal, you didn't order it, you didn't sit mulling over the decision of what to have, excited to have options on whatever you want. You were tied to that chair in the restaurant bounded by chains and force fed a three-course meal of emotions you didn't want to swallow.

None of them tasted good, grief being the hardest one to swallow, you still haven't accepted it after all these years and that's the one that sits in your stomach and causes you the most issues, it heightens all the other emotions because it's the one that stings the most, it's a bitter taste that once induced it won't ever go away.

You can try to cover it up by eating huge amounts of happiness and trying your hardest to mask the flavour, but it's destined to always come through. You can be walking along one day, and you smell something that takes you back years, back to that meal and every sense in your body is awakened. It makes you sad because you want the control of being able to deal with it, but you just can't. You wonder every day, if you had just eaten the starter and been spared the rest of the meal would you be the person you are today. Would you be different, would it be easier to cover up the gut-wrenching sadness that lives inside of you? It's survival, you tell yourself, you have to eat to live, you have to learn to overcome it all, and just when you think you have a hold on it, you slip.

The end result is you no longer eat out, instead you starve yourself of any emotions you could taste.

Trolls

When I was a child, I always recall fairy tale books which contained trolls. These hideous creatures that lurk around awaiting to pounce on you when you least expect it. They are ugly on the inside and out, the main purpose of a troll is to upset and destroy the happy ever after to the story.

Well, I always thought growing up that I would outgrow this fear and realise this was alas just a fairy tale that scared me when I was small, and it was ok because they didn't exist, it was all pretend and I had no reason to ever worry about coming across trolls in my life, except in a storybook.

How wrong was I? that actually the trolls have now taken over. The mystery still surrounds them as we never actually see their ugliness, instead we endure their harsh words and insults over social networking, they have now taken over the internet as the bridge they hide under and succeed in dragging people down and spoiling the happy ever afters they are all aiming for.

I wonder how many children read these stories and aspired to grow up to become that troll, all the children loathed so much in the story.

My Ambitions in life Vs my friends

Friend-get a flashy car that consists of half of their income being paid out on it every month

Mine-get a car that's newer than 1901, it starts in winter and it isn't leaking oil constantly

Friend-get promotion after promotion at work

Mine-actually have an average job where I don't lay in bed on a Sunday night, thinking of all the illnesses I can contract so I don't have to go in on Monday

Friend-get married and have the most exclusive wedding day that they will spend the rest of their life paying off

Mine-just attend other people's weddings, for the cake

Friend-get a mortgage on a big fancy house, where all your friends are envious of your new home

Mine-get a rented house where my neighbours don't have 10 screaming children, or the couple don't have orgy's every night of the week

Friend-earn lots and lots of money

Mine-a lifetime supply of crunchy Cheetos is richness to me

Friend-have 3 or 4 kids

Mine-have 19 dogs, so I can name them all the days of the week and months of the year

Friend-to have wardrobes full of designer clothes

Mine-for it to be acceptable to turn up to work in pyjamas

Friend-to be successful

Mine-success is completing candy crush

Friend-to have botox regular

Mine-to have money for the January sales

Friend-to own every item Apple sells

Mine-to try and add an apple into my daily intake diet

Friend-go to the Caribbean and spend 10 days in a hammock

Mine-getting a flight on Ryan Air for £9.99

Friend-mass shopping days out, where spending their wages doesn't make them blink

Mine-spending £10 on eBay without using my overdraft

Friend-get pumped up at the gym, feel the burn and see that muscle form

Mine-to not get thrush from the uncomfortable bike seat during spinning class

About The Author

Penelope Bond (known as Penny) studied a BA in American Studies, followed by an MA in Journalism.

Her writing style is conversationalist and is usually personal to her in some way. She's a huge fan of film, dogs, travel and breakfast food. She is not a fan of tin foil or early morning alarm calls.

One of her biggest achievements was receiving a British Empire Medal for her volunteer work. One of her not so biggest achievements is despite her age, she still hasn't mastered how to cook a proper meal.

High strung and a bit wild   Penny J Bond

Books by this author

Letting go of the rain

From childhood to adulthood, one girl learns about understanding Complex Post-Traumatic Stress Disorder, and finally it all makes so much sense to her.

Her imposter syndrome, her triggers, her emotional flashbacks, the way her emotions are. She always thought it was just her, that she hadn't grieved properly and that she herself had somehow ignited her own self destructive behaviour, always thinking she deserves nothing good in life.

She shares her experiences in the form of letters she writes to her dad over the years, who's death was the biggest trauma of all for her.

"I feel sad when it rains, it controls my emotions and my mood. Sometimes I sit by my bedroom window on those rainy days, when the sky is grey and that rumbling sound echoes above from the sky and I run my finger down the window pane trying to touch the rain through the glass telling myself I have nothing to fear, but still that haunting feeling is there".

The book shares an honest account of a child's journey experiencing grief, trauma and guilt, into adulthood.

Tired Bones

A collection of pieces about love, life, laughter and loss.

A tattered teddy, the moon, the lovers and the candle of life are among the things that have been twisted into some short thought provoking pieces to inhale.......

If the wind could talk what would it say...?

Its Ruby & Honey, Ruby gets a surprise

This is the first story in a series of adventures of two furry four legged doggy friends called Ruby and Honey. In this edition Ruby has been the only family pet for a long time, but she's about to get a surprise in the form of a new friend called Honey. Ruby is unsure how to feel and feels sad and a little lost, she thinks she may get pushed out now there is a new family member. The series of stories highlights emotions and feelings we all experience only these stories are told through the eyes of our doggy friends.

Its Ruby & Honey, Honey loves her monster

This is the second story in the "It's Ruby & Honey" collection. Honey loves her monster, she's with it nearly every second of the day, but what happens if she can't find it? why does she get angry with Ruby if she touches it? and what is it about this soft pink monster that makes her love it as much as she does.This is a tale about the things that can mean the world to us, only this tale is told through the eyes of our fluffy four legged friend....Honey.

Printed in Great Britain
by Amazon